TEARS OF RAGE

Part One:

First Chosen

Garrett

Happy birthday

Hope you enjoy

A Novel By:

M Todd Gallowglas

M Todd

First Chosen

Cover design Ed Litfin

First Printing October 2011
8 7 6 5 4 3 2 1 0 9

Books by M. Todd Gallowglas:

TEARS OF RAGE
First Chosen
Once We Were Like Wolves
Arms of the Storm
Judge of Dooms
*Fires of Night**

Halloween Jack and the Devil's Gate
Halloween Jack and the Curse of Frost
Halloween Jack and the Red Emperor *

"The Dragon Bone Flute"
"Legacy of the Dragon Bone Flute"
"Jaludin's Road"

* Forthcoming

Praise for First Chosen

"This is really great stuff! The characters seem real, three dimensional people, not typical fantasy types." – James Rollins, Author of THE DEVIL COLONY and MAP OF BONES.

"The pacing kept me engaged, and I have to admit, kept me up past my bedtime on more than one occasion. I can't wait to read the sequel." - Shay Fabbro, author of *THE PORTALS OF DESTINY*

"I wish I could write fight scenes like that." Jen Wylie, Author of *SWEET LIGHT*

"The characters are well-drawn and the world is truly fascinating, with its talk of gods and miracles. It is an unconventional design for a fantasy novel, and it works very much to the author's advantage… *First Chosen* is one of my top 5 favorite books of 2011!" - Christopher Kellen, author of *ELEGY* and *THE CORPSE KING*

"M. Todd Gallowglas has written a compelling tale in *First Chosen (Tears of Rage)*. The world in which he sets the tale is a vivid, complex world; one in which theology and politics are so intertwined that it is hard to tell where one leaves off and the other begins." - Best in Fantasy Blog

"The storytelling was truly out of this world. Gallowglas has created something gorgeous and complex." - Diana @Offbeat Vagabond.

"*First Chosen* isn't just a book - it is a window into another world." - Merelan Jones, *Renaissance Productions*

"*First Chosen* is a complex story, multi-layered and containing a rich mythology and large amount of world building. I was impressed with the word that Gallowglas has apparently put into creating not only his world, but its various cultures, mythologies, religions and even languages. The rich interactions of his characters fill the story with a sense that you know these people and you grow to care very much what happens to them. K. Sozaeva "Obsessive Bibliophile"

For Robin
Without her, there wouldn't be a Julianna.

Acknowledgements

I would like to thank the following people for their continuous support in this journey I started on when I was a little boy and first realized I wanted to tell stories through the written word: My dad for getting me the very first fantasy novel, and then getting me even more despite the fact I don't think he understood the obsession. My mom, for giving me permission to dream as big as I wanted. Damon Stone, for dreaming big with me and also helping to keep me from getting lost in those dreams. Aunt Penny, for getting it and calling me on my crap. Jim Czajkowski and Dave Meek, for believing that I had it in me. Steve Moore, Pat "Snipe" Ruele, and Trey Cromwell for letting me play in the cool kids' club. Bill Watters and Marti Miernik for giving me a venue to build the best fan base a storyteller could hope to have. Steven Erikson, who taught me how far I could push the envelope of fantasy fiction. Matthew Clark Davidson and Alice La Plante, the two teachers who demanded more of my story-telling than anyone else, before or since; I've tried to live up to your expectations. Ashlin Ferguson, for keeping me from going out in public with my fly down. Ed Litfin, for the awesome cover.

Finally, Robert and Mathew, for being the coolest kids in the world.

Dramatis Personæ

The Komati

Julianna Taraen – A duchess celebrating her twenty-first birthday.
Alyxandros Vivaen – A count. Julianna's uncle.
Maerie Vivaen – A countess. Wife of Alyxandros. Julianna's aunt on her father's side.
Khellan Dubhan – A baron, suitor to Julianna
Ingram Dashette – A viscount, friend of Khellan.
Jansyn Collaen – A baronet, friend of Khellan.
Sophya Mandak – Julianna's friend.
Perrine Raelle – Julianna's friend.
Sylvie Raelle – Perinne's little sister.
Bryce Anssi – A drunk

Kingdom of the Sun

Octavio Salvatore – Kingdom Governor of Koma
Dante Salvatore – Octavio's younger brother
Hardin Thorinson – Adept of Old Uncle Night.
Carmine D'Mario – Half-blood noble both of the House Floraen and of Komati blood.
Nicco D'Mario – Carmine's younger brother
Luciano Salvatore – House Floraen Inquisitor
Santo Salvatore – House Floraen Inquisitor
Roark – Adept of Old Uncle Night

Commoners

Raenard – A Komati soldier
Maerik – A Komati soldier
Saeryn – A Komati soldier
Theordon Barristis – Man at arms to Alyxandros Vivaen
Colette – Julianna's maid
Faelin vara'Traejyn – a bastard wanderer
Jorgen – A Kingdom soldier

Celestials, Infernals, and Others

Grandfather Shadow – Known also as Galad'Ysoysa. A Greater God.
Yrgaeshkil – The Mother of Daemyns, Goddess of Lies.
Kahddria – Goddess of Wind
Skaethak – Goddess of Winter

Innaya – An Aengyl
Kaeldyr the Gray – a Saent of Grandfather Shadow
Nae'Toran'borlahisth – A Daemyn
Razka – A Stormseeker
The King of Order
The Lords of Judgment
Maxian
Kavala

PROLOGUE

Why do people consider being touched by divine powers to be a blessing? – Talmoinan the White

She will come to the world when man and Daemyn fight together against the heavens. Born of wolf's cunning and man's wit, she will be blessed thrice by seven, seven by thrice. Once those blessings are spent, her anguish will give truth to what she forgot. – Attributed to the Blind Prophet

ONE

Blessed by Once

In the moments before Julianna's birth, Kaeldyr flew on wings of shadow toward the one chance to save his god. His flight through the spirit world was a calculated balance of speed and stealth. He had only remained undetected this long by traveling in hidden corners of the World Between Worlds; however, he would have to interact with the mortal realm soon. Once that happened, his intentions could no longer remain hidden. Then the celestial powers would intervene.

Even though it was the middle of the night when Kaeldyr arrived at the manor house, everyone in the household was wide awake. Servants scurried through the hallways. The lady of the house was with child, and her labor pains had started earlier that day. Even the barrier between worlds barely muffled the noise as her cries echoed through the halls. In the physical realm she must have been deafening.

Entering the birthing room, Kaeldyr looked down upon the lady. The sheets clung to her sweat-soaked body. Her eyes, deep gray like a storm rolling in from an angry sea, blinked through the tears. A midwife sat next to the lady's head. She whispered to the lady in a calming voice and dabbed the lady's forehead with a wet cloth. Another midwife sat at the far end of the bed, swaddling clothes ready. Surrounding each of the midwives, Kaeldyr saw a nimbus of light, shifting and multicolored, revealing the strength and age of their souls. Despite the physical age of their current lives, both possessed relatively young souls. The oldest of them had only been reborn five times. The light of the lady's soul was different, as her kind only had one life. Where the midwives' souls were rainbows of bright, vibrant colors, the lady's soul was shades of blue, gray, and white.

Looking past the flaring emotions of the lady and the two midwives, Kaeldyr saw the reason he'd come: a fourth soul in the room, the lady's unborn child, a soul who had never seen life. The baby's soul was nearly pure white, with edges of blue and gray. This unborn child, unscarred by the cycle of life, death, and rebirth, possessed nearly infinite potential and possibility. As it was with souls born into the world for the first time, this child would possess a strength of spirit unknown by all but a few. No matter what path these children took, their lives almost always changed the world.

This child was going to free Kaeldyr's god, Grandfather Shadow.

Pushing his finger through the woman's abdomen, Kaeldyr touched the unborn soul. In all his centuries as a celestial being, Kaeldyr had never done such a thing. Touching this soul was like tasting sweetened fruit tea, smelling a rose, and listening to a mother's lullaby – all through his fingers. As he probed the soul, he felt like it – no, not it, *she*; this was definitely a girl – she examined him in return. The sweetness that Kaeldyr felt turned slightly salty, though not enough to be unpleasant. She seemed to be asking, *What are you?*

He smiled, drew on his faith, and whispered in Grandfather Shadow's divine language, speaking a miracle. Written words formed in the air as Kaeldyr spoke, the letters appearing in the spider-web scrawl of Grandfather Shadow's alphabet. The words hung in the air for a moment, then floated down and settled into the unborn girl's soul. Even with all the divine powers Grandfather Shadow had bestowed upon him as Saent Kaeldyr the Gray, Kaeldyr chose to use the power of miracle, a power available only to humans. Within moments, all but the faintest shred of his faith belonged to the girl. His faith would lie buried deep in the folds of the girl's dreams, waiting for her moment of greatest need. When that moment came, she would release Grandfather Shadow from his imprisonment.

"Stop!" shouted a voice behind him.

"*Mina suoda, Thanya'taen,*" Kaeldyr spoke the miracle and summoned the ancient sword to his free hand.

The sword was long and thin, forged of a metal that mortals had come to call Faerii steel. The hilt was bound in black leather and silver wire. It was long enough to be used with two hands, but the blade was thin and light enough that the wielder could fight one-handed if he chose. Runes in Grandfather Shadow's divine language had been etched into the lower half of the blade, declaring the weapon's name.

Thanya'taen. Tears of Rage.

Kaeldyr turned.

Three Aengyls stood facing him, appearing mostly human but for their feathered wings, taloned feet, and bird-like heads. The closest Aengyl had the head of a great horned owl. Two with the heads of eagles flanked it. They regarded him with eyes that glowed pure white. Each held a sword of shining light.

"Saent Kaeldyr," said the owl-headed Aengyl, "the King of Order commands you to step aside."

"No."

A moment later, Stormseekers in wolf form and Stormcrows in avian form surrounded him, growling and cawing their defiance. These Faerii creatures bound to Grandfather Shadow formed a wall between Kaeldyr and the Aengyls.

So long as the girl was unborn, her soul could be sent into the Dark Realm of the Godless Dead to be cast outside the cycle of life, death, and rebirth. Her body would be stillborn, and Kaeldyr's faith would evaporate, sacrificed for nothing. Kaeldyr had to hold them until the child was born. After that, the ancient treaty between the King of Order, the Lords of Judgment, and the Princes of Chaos would protect the girl.

"You have one chance to avoid punishment," the owl said. "Stand aside."

"No."

The Aengyls raised their swords. Kaeldyr smiled and tightened his grip on *Thanya'taen.* He had been waiting for this moment since the Battle of Ykthae Wood.

"Attack," he said.

The Stormcrows flew in first, lightning sparkling along their talons. They did not damage the Aengyls, but they weren't meant to. They were only a distraction. After the tempest of talons, wings, and feathers, the Stormseekers followed, snapping at the Aengyl's arms, legs, and wings.

In the midst of that assault, Kaeldyr dove to his right and lunged forward. He brought his sword up, severing an eagle-headed Aengyl's sword arm. White light shone from the amputated limb. A screech pierced through the spirit world, and Kaeldyr knew he wouldn't get in another lucky shot.

Ducking under a cut from the owl-headed Aengyl, Kaeldyr spun, blocked a second cut aimed at his head, and lashed out with a counter. His blade nearly sliced into the Aengyl's neck. At the last moment, the Aengyl's wing flapped up, blocking Kaeldyr's blow. Sword and wing met, producing a shower of feathers.

The Stormseekers darted in and out of the third Aengyl's sword range, keeping him from joining the fight against Kaeldyr.

The one-armed Aengyl rushed in under Kaeldyr's guard and grappled him around the hips. Not bothering to try and free himself, Kaeldyr parried the owl's attacks. He didn't need to win. He only needed to last a few more moments.

The eagle grappling with him plunged its beak into Kaeldyr's side. He screamed as pain burned through him. The owl took advantage of that opening and thrust its sword at Kaeldyr's head.

Another sword – a black blade that pulsed with a cold sickness – came out of nowhere and parried the Aengyl's blow. Something pulled away the Aengyl on Kaeldyr's waist. A Daemyn stood next to him, sword of black flames dancing in its hand. It smiled and beckoned to the Aengyls.

Kaeldyr recognized the newcomer. Leathery wings rose from its back, and ram's horns sprouted from behind its bat-like ears. Its short name was Nae'Toran. Kaeldyr had fought the creature several times in the Second War of the Gods, finally defeating and humiliating him at the Battle of Ykthae Wood. Nae'Toran launched himself at the Aengyls, and Kaeldyr followed; there was no time to question the Daemyn's presence now. With this creature's help, there was a greater chance to see the girl born.

Kaeldyr, the Stormseekers, Stormcrows, and the Daemyn fought hard against the Aengyls, but their numbers kept dwindling.

When more than half the wolves and crows were down, a voice came from the physical world, "It's a girl."

A moment later, the baby cried for the first time.

Now that the mortal world was affected, the King of Order could not change it.

"Name her Julianna," the mother gasped, "after Saent Julian the Courageous."

Kaeldyr hoped Julianna grew up to have more in common with Saent Julian than just a name. The girl would need all of Julian's bravery, and more.

"You failed," Kaeldyr said.

As Kaeldyr felt himself being pulled from the spirit world back into the celestial realms, he threw *Thanya'taen* away. He could not let anyone who was not a follower of Grandfather Shadow come to possess that weapon. Nae'Toran scrambled for it, but a large Stormcrow, larger than an eagle, snatched the weapon and flew down a path into the deep spirit, where the Daemyn couldn't follow.

"You have broken the celestial decree of the Ykthae Accord!" came a chorus of voices. The Lords of Judgment spoke as one. They were the Incarnates who maintained a balance of power between the King of Order, Princes of Chaos, and the Queen of Passion.

"I did," Kaeldyr said.

"You will be punished!"

"I am ready."

First they removed his word – *the Gray* – that Grandfather Shadow had blessed him with so many centuries ago. They ripped it from him without ceremony or trial. Without it, he was no longer a Saent, just a mortal husk in the celestial realms. His body aged to the state it had been in when he died: old, frail, and broken. It didn't matter, because then they shredded his body to nothing in the span of a heartbeat. He would have screamed, but he no longer had lungs or throat. Kaeldyr felt something caress his soul, the only piece of him that remained. It was Nae'Toran.

"They have given you to me as a warning to others who might follow in your footsteps." The Daemyn's smile held no warmth. "Your punishment is being my plaything until I am done with you, then your soul can rot away wherever I decide to drop it."

Then Kaeldyr, Grandfather Shadow's first high priest, named at the moment of his first death, Saent Kaeldyr the Gray, was removed completely from the cycle of life, death, and rebirth – exiled to the Dark Realm of the Godless Dead.

TWO

The spirit world was quiet. The lady's labor cries had ended with the birth of her daughter. The battle between the Saents, Aengyls, and Daemyns had chased away any spirits that might have taken residence here. In this silence, Yrgaeshkil, wife of Old Uncle Night and mother of all Daemyns, lowered the Lie that hid her from the sight of men and Eldar, those beings that mortals called gods. This evening, she wore the form of one of her children, even though she despised it. She had a bat's head with deer's horns, and she wrapped her leathery wings about her shoulders like a cloak.

Nae'Toran bowed before her.

"It is done, Mother," her son said. "Soon you will be able to take your rightful place among the celestial hierarchy."

Yrgaeshkil was a Lesser Eldar, with command over but a single dominion, the dominion of Lies; however, she wanted more. No, she *needed* more. The desire for it burned in her the way she imagined that mortals desired sex and strong drink. She had instigated two wars that had raged throughout all the realms in her quest to command more Dominions and achieve a place among the Greater Eldar.

At the very end of the Second War, Yrgaeshkil had finally gained a second dominion, and then promptly lost it again. This had been the greatest stroke of luck any being, celestial, infernal, or mortal had ever received. Shortly after Yrgaeshkil had lost her second dominion, the King of Order had imprisoned the five Greater Eldar. Had she maintained control of that second dominion, she would have been imprisoned too. Several of the other Lesser Eldar had argued that Yrgaeshkil should be imprisoned as well, but the King of Order could only abide by the letter of his decree, no matter what the spirit of that decree was.

"How long will you wait before forcing the child to use Kaeldyr's gift?" Nae'Toran asked.

"Seven years should be sufficient."

"Seven years? Why so long?"

Yrgaeshkil shook her head. Even with all his centuries of existence, her son still had not learned patience.

"Seven is a number sacred to Grandfather Shadow, and since Kaeldyr's faith is attuned to that god, it seems appropriate. The girl will need to grow old enough to learn about Grandfather Shadow. I've waited nearly a thousand years for circumstances to be this perfect. I can wait a little while longer."

Yrgaeshkil peered between the worlds as the lady nursed her daughter, her little Julianna. The pure, near-white of the girl's soul shone between the worlds, declaring her strength to any creature who knew what to look for. Yes, this Julianna was going to change everything.

THREE

Blessed by Twice

The night before her seventh birthday, Julianna woke up. It wasn't the slow waking that came naturally in the morning, with the sunlight peeking through the curtains. This was a quick waking in the middle of the night, the kind of waking that came when the nightmares grew too much for her to bear, when those eyes wouldn't stop staring at her from within the darkness of her mind's eye. However, this time, the nightmares hadn't come, and those eyes had been absent from her mind more and more.

Her room was dark. Moonlight shone through the small space between her curtains making a ghostly line of white in the middle of her black floor.

She heard voices downstairs. Did Mother and Father have guests? She didn't recall a formal supper being planned, and while her parents' friends would occasionally surprise them with an evening visit, it would be unusual for them to stay this late.

Perhaps Mother and Father were speaking to Julianna's nurse, preparing her for the next day when the nurse's services would no longer be needed. Julianna smiled at the thought of that conversation. After tomorrow, Julianna would never have to suffer her nurse – who she always thought of as *that woman* – again.

Footsteps echoed throughout the house, and Julianna thought she heard the fourth step of the main stairs creak. It had been like that for years, and both Mother and Father refused to get it fixed. The stair creaked again, and again. Someone said something. Julianna couldn't understand the words, but the tone sounded like Father speaking to one of his followers who had disobeyed him.

A gunshot sounded. Julianna tensed so much that her heart seemed to stop. Her breath came in quick in-and-out blasts through clenched teeth. This wasn't the first time someone attacked the house, and it wouldn't be the last – Father and Mother had many enemies throughout the Kingdom – but this was the first time anyone had ever fired a gun in the manor.

Firearms were illegal; possessing one was a capital offense in the Kingdom of the Sun. The estate had never been as quiet as it was in the few moments that followed that gunshot. Another gunshot sounded, and fighting broke the silence. Julianna's heart sped up as if it needed to catch those beats it had lost in the silence. She gripped her blankets and pulled the covers over her head.

The door opened. She held her breath and tightened every part of her body to be perfectly still. The door closed. She bit her lip to keep quiet.

"Julianna?" Mother's voice whispered from the other side of the blanket.

Julianna leapt from her bed. "Mother? I heard gunshots. Are they in the house?"

"Help me with the sheets," Mother said.

Together they stripped the bed. All the while fighting continued in other parts of the house. Steel clashed. Gunshots rang out. Mother made a long rope out of the sheets, tied one end to the foot of Julianna's wardrobe, and tossed the other end out the window. Julianna took a step toward the window, but Mother grabbed her and pushed her under the bed. A moment later, Mother joined her amongst the dust, forgotten toys, and spiders.

"Take this, Julianna," Mother said. "It will protect you against anything less than a god."

Mother pushed something into Julianna's hands. She looked down. It was one of Father's knives. The blade was nearly as long as her arm and twice as wide as her thumb. It had a single word etched into the blade in the language of the god Mother and Father worshipped.

Kostota.

"Listen to me, Julianna," Mother whispered. Mother only used Julianna's proper name when she was angry or very serious. Any other time, Julianna was *Little Duchess.* "If they find us, I want you to fight. Fight like the forty-nine Morigahnti at the Battle of Ykthae Wood. Fight to make your father proud. Fight hard enough to make them kill you." Mother shook Julianna's shoulders. "Do you understand me? Do not let them take you while you live."

Julianna nodded and gripped her weapon. "I understand."

"Now quiet," Mother said.

Julianna buried her face in Mother's shoulder.

They waited. Julianna couldn't tell how long. She tried to track the time by counting her heartbeats but lost count well before one hundred.

Eventually, the sounds of fighting diminished. Julianna tried to crawl out from under the bed. Mother grabbed her and pulled her tighter. Footsteps echoed on the upper floor. They came closer and closer. The door opened and light spilled in. People came into Julianna's room. She couldn't help but glance at their feet. She saw between six and eight pairs of legs.

"They're gone."

"Check the wardrobe."

Both voices belonged to men.

Feet moved across the floor. She heard her wardrobe doors open, and her favorite outfits started to fall on the floor.

"Adept," another voice said. "The sheets aren't long enough to reach to the ground safely."

They would check under the bed next, Julianna knew it. Her breath quickened as she imagined what horrors these men intended. Julianna squirmed out of Mother's grasp and slid out from under the foot of her bed. There hadn't been any feet there, and the men wouldn't be able to see her crouched low. Julianna decided the dumbwaiter was their only chance. Mother could fit inside of it if she squeezed.

A hand closed on Julianna's shoulder and yanked her back. She shifted her grip on the knife like Father had shown her. She jabbed backward with the blade, and the air in front of her shimmered with motes of silver light. A wolf appeared from out of that light and leapt over Julianna's head. Julianna didn't have to look back when she heard a gurgled cry to know the wolf had clasped its jaws onto the man's throat.

Julianna scrambled for her escape. Another hand grabbed her, this time by her hair. The strong grip nearly pulled her off her feet.

Julianna gritted her teeth and sucked in a deep breath that cooled her mouth. She reached out for the dumbwaiter with her mind, she thought about being there a few moments ago. There was a flash of silver light, and then Julianna was next to the dumbwaiter.

She scrambled inside. Looking back, she saw a figure in black hardened-leather armor with an oversized skull for the helmet. The Brotherhood of the Night. Father's most hated enemies, and servants of the God of Death, Old Uncle Night. The terrifying figure held onto her past self, but paused when he saw her double appear at the dumbwaiter. Julianna watched herself sink the knife into her attacker's leg. Then a wolf appeared in a shower of light and ripped out the attacker's throat.

Flashes of light appeared throughout the room, and the she-wolf seemed to be everywhere at once. Then three more Nightbrothers ran into the room carrying staves made of some silver metal. They struck the staves together, and a brilliant light shone in the room. It was so bright Julianna had to look away.

When she looked back, the she-wolf was gone, and the men in black armor held Mother pinned to the floor. Mother tried to move, tried to shift through the world as Julianna had done. A nimbus of silvery light formed around her, but the three staves came together, the room filled with light again, and Mother remained trapped. Julianna started out of the dumbwaiter.

"No!" Mother screamed. "Run! Find your father."

Julianna pulled on the rope inside the waiter as hard as she could.

"Let her go," the man said. "She won't go far. Besides, it's the husband we want. Get her clothes off and he'll find us."

Laughter echoed behind those skull masks.

Julianna knew she could call for help. Something from deep in that place where she remembered her dreams hours or days later told her she had someone who would help her. She wanted to speak the words, but couldn't. She could only ask once, and the help had to be for her and only for her.

Instead, she locked eyes with the one who looked like the leader, the only one without a white skull masking his face.

"My father's god is going to eat your soul!" Julianna yelled as she hurried downward.

FOUR

Yrgaeshkil wanted to scream. She paced back and forth in the darkness of a copse of trees watching the battle raging around the manor house. Morigahnti, the followers of Grandfather Shadow, fought against the Brotherhood of the Night. Even though the Brotherhood warriors outnumbered the Morigahnti more than three to one, the battle was going against the Brotherhood. They did not have the advantage of firearms, and only one in six or so of the Brotherhood could channel divine power as miracles, whereas nearly half of the Morigahnti could.

She wanted to kill someone. No. She specifically wanted to kill the scarred-faced man standing next to her. But she couldn't. Kavala was a necessary component of too many of her schemes. Even if she didn't need him, Yrgaeshkil wasn't sure she could contain her power in her current mood. Getting noticed wandering around the physical realm was the last thing she wanted.

Somehow, Julianna had managed to escape the initial attack. The girl had gotten out of the building, and her grandfather had spirited her away to who knew where or even when. It couldn't be too far. The girl's human blood would make shifting her over too great a distance impossible, but a Stormseeker could still travel beyond reach very quickly in a series of rapid, short jumps.

The only consolation to this failure was the Morigahnti corpses that littered the ground outside the manor; unfortunately, this was countered by an even greater number of her husband's followers. While Yrgaeshkil didn't actually care about these mortals in the greater scheme, she needed them for the time being as she built her own powerbase.

Yrgaeshkil turned to the man known as Kavala. "You promised me it would happen."

Even though the left side of his face was a mangled mass of cuts and scars, she could see the boredom in the way his gaze would not quite meet hers and how his shoulders rocked slightly back and forth.

"It should have," he replied, looking past her to the house. "I cannot control the men if they attack the wrong person, especially from out here. I recall wanting to lead the attack myself."

"It matters not," Yrgaeshkil snarled through her teeth. "In seven years, I will ensure that she calls him forth."

FIVE

Blessed by Thrice

Julianna should have been celebrating her fourteenth birthday. She should have been treated to one of the finest meals of her life, danced with handsome and powerful young lords, and been introduced to all the other nobles of House Kolmonen and their allies. These thoughts plagued her – should-haves and could-haves dancing about her in feverish visions.

A fire burned in the hearth of Julianna's bedroom, but its heat could not compare to the fever that burned inside of her. She lay wrapped in thick down blankets to help protect her from the chill of an early winter. Sometimes in Koma, the autumn storms came in midsummer, which brought winter early. Having snow storms in summer was rare, but not unheard of. This early winter had also brought sickness.

Julianna slid her hand under the pillow and gripped the hilt of her mother's dagger. Even though it had been under her pillow for days, the hilt was still cool to the touch. It was the only thing Julianna possessed that had belonged to either of her parents. Sometimes, late at night, she would stare at the weapon by candlelight and try and decipher the single word etched into either side of the blade, *Kostota*. She felt as though there had been a time when she had known what that word meant, but like so many things from before the fire killed her parents, she couldn't seem to remember, no matter how hard she tried.

Faces swam above her bed: Mother with her piercing gray eyes, Father with the scar that ran down his face, and her cousins. Her cousins were gone, just like her parents. The fever had not addled Julianna so much that she could not hear a death bell ring twice in the last week. The first time it rang, it sounded twenty-three times for Marcus's age. The second time, two days later, it rang sixteen times for Raechel.

Nobody had told Julianna about their deaths. She knew because no one mentioned Marcus or Raechel in her presence. Once, Julianna had asked after her cousins. "Just worry about resting," was the reply, "everything will be fine."

The bells would ring for her next, unless some miracle saved her. At the thought of a miracle, all the faces vanished. A pair of dark eyes replaced them. She didn't remember much before she came to live with her aunt and uncle, but she felt that those eyes had always been with her, just like the words that swam in the back of her mind, words that she could speak and receive aid. She didn't know what form the aid would take, and she'd never wanted to ask for it, because for some reason, she felt that she could only call for that help once.

Well, she was about to die. If she was ever going to satisfy her curiosity, she would have to take that offer of help now. She licked her lips. She hadn't spoken a word in days. Just as she began to form the first syllable, the door opened. The light from the hall hurt Julianna's eyes. She let go of the knife to shield her eyes.

Two people entered. She recognized Uncle Alyx's short and wiry silhouette. As usual when he was at home, Uncle Alyx wore his hair down and the graying strands fell around his shoulders. The other man was more than a head taller than Uncle Alyx. Even in the dim light from the hall, Julianna saw that he wore tan leathers and furs like the wild Dosahan to the west.

The stranger came right up to Julianna's bed and leaned over her.

"I'm glad that you were able to come," Uncle Alyx said. "This sickness has taken so many already."

"I'm sorry I couldn't be here in time to help Marcus and Raechel." The man's voice sounded familiar.

"The fault is mine for not thinking of you sooner," Uncle Alyx said. "I was too lost in my own grief."

"Your family was dying around you," the other man said. "I understand how that can cloud your thinking." The other man looked Julianna over. "She is bad, but it's not too late. Julianna, you have to drink this."

The man slid his hand under the pillow. He lifted her head, and the room swam in Julianna's vision. Something touched her lips, a cup or bowl of some kind. She sniffed at it. It smelled like spoiled beer mixed with seaweed. Her stomach tightened. She clamped her lips shut between her teeth and tried to turn her head away.

"Colette," the man said. "Hold her head."

Colette had been Raechel's maid.

A pair of small, cool hands grasped each side of Julianna's head. There was not much strength in them, but in her sickened state Julianna could not free herself. Another hand, this one rough and calloused, covered her nose. Again, the vessel containing the nauseating concoction came to her lips and pushed its way between them. The liquid scalded her tongue. She tried to spit it out, but another calloused hand covered her mouth. She could swallow or choke. She swallowed.

The rough hands released her, and she gasped for breath.

"She must drink a mouthful of this every five hours," the man said. "Then she will live."

"Yes, my lord," Colette replied.

There was a flutter of wind in Julianna's room, and then the man was gone.

"Watch over her, Colette," Uncle Alyx said.

"Yes, my lord," Colette replied with a curtsy.

Once Uncle Alyx left the room, Colette sat on the edge of the bed. Julianna heard soft splashes next to the bed. A moment later, a damp cloth touched her brow.

"Don't worry, my lady," Colette's soft voice said. "I'll take care of you."

"Julianna." Julianna's voice came out in a whisper through her dry throat.

"Excuse me, my lady?"

Julianna swallowed. It didn't help much. "When we're alone together," she took a breath, "call me Julianna."

"Yes, my…" Colette paused, as if speaking a noble's proper name was a blasphemy she dared not risk. "Julianna." After a moment, she spoke again, "Julianna," this time with more courage. "We'll see you though this, Julianna."

SIX

Yrgaeshkil stepped to the side, fleeing the room where Julianna had again failed to call for aid in what should have been her most desperate moment. The Goddess of Lies appeared in her husband's throne room and collapsed into the throne of bones and dried human flesh. She had fled in fear, but not the fear that something ill might befall her. Yrgaeshkil fled because she feared that she might kill Julianna. Yrgaeshkil needed the girl alive if she ever hoped to gain more dominions. This plan would not likely work a second time.

There was a commotion in the throne room. Yrgaeshkil looked up.

Daemyns scurried this way and that, heading for the tunnels that led out of the throne room. Well, it wouldn't be as satisfying as killing the girl, but it might help her mood a bit. She let out a howl full of such fury that it shredded several of the slower creatures. She looked at the mangled, bloody remains and sighed. It hadn't helped.

"I take it that the sickness failed, Mother," Nae'Toran asked. He had wisely remained next to the throne, out of her direct sight.

"Yes," Yrgaeshkil said.

The illness had been a calculated risk – much riskier than any other part of her plan had been. She had drawn on her husband's power over the dominion of Sickness. If she'd used even a breath more of it, the King of Order might have accused her of usurping the dominion and imprisoned her for becoming a Greater Eldar.

"What am I going to do?" Her wailing voice echoed throughout the throne room.

"Might I make a suggestion, Mother?" Nae'Toran asked.

"Speak."

Nae'Toran told her his plan.

"Yes. Yes, of course. You are the only one who has managed to get anything right in this scheme. In seven years, I will send you to finish what you started. But do not fail me."

"Never, Mother," Nae'Toran said. "I am no flawed mortal. She will speak the words. And you will know your heart's desire at long last."

CELEBRATION OF BIRTH

The moment the greater gods were imprisoned was the first moment mankind commanded its own destiny. – Talmoinan the White

Grandfather Shadow would rather have you defiant and full of cunning rather than meek and obedient in your faith. Let the other followers have their mindless drones who worship any words a priest gives to them. The other gods wish to be considered great by their followers. Grandfather Shadow wishes to be considered for his followers' greatness. – Kaeldyr, the first Lord Morigahn

ONE

Julianna sat at breakfast on the morning of her twenty-first birthday, the traditional day of Komati adulthood, and just as with the sickness when she was fourteen, the gods threatened to take this day from her as well – unless, of course, Julianna defied the gods. And why shouldn't she? It was her life, her memories of a day she would carry until she died.

Julianna leaned forward, clutched both hands to her stomach, and made a gagging sound. At the other end of the table, Aunt Maerie nibbled on carefully cut bits of pastries while Uncle Alyxandros sipped at his tea and read a letter. Breakfast had been a simple affair, consisting of porridge, fruits, and tea. They had to save room for all the food at the introduction supper when Julianna would officially meet Duke Martyn Collaen, a boorish oaf of a man who had expressed interest in a political marriage between Julianna and himself.

"What better way to enter into the adult world," Aunt Maerie had said, "than to accept the hand of one of the wealthiest and most powerful men in Koma."

The thought of being courted by Duke Martyn, a man nearly twice Julianna's twenty-one years, made her stomach churn. She gripped the table with her right hand, and groaned, "Gods and goddesses."

Aunt Maerie's fork stopped halfway between the plate and her mouth. She set the fork down without as much as a *clink* on the plate and folded her hands together. Her lips formed a thin line as her face tightened so that Julianna could see every one of the worry lines in the old woman's face – lines that Aunt Maerie claimed came from watching over Julianna. Uncle Alyxandros looked up from his letter. His gaze met Julianna's, and she thought she saw the left corner of his mouth creep up a bit. As always, she could gain no insight from his deep brown eyes.

"Julianna." Aunt Maerie stared straight ahead and her lips barely moved. She spoke in the same, almost singsong tone she used when her undersized dogs wouldn't perform their tricks properly for guests. "I won't tolerate that language at—"

"Maerie," Uncle Alyxandros said.

"Alyx, do not attempt to defend her—"

Uncle Alyxandros cleared his throat, cutting off Aunt Maerie's protests. She opened her mouth, but he waved his letter toward Julianna. The instant she had Aunt Maerie's attention, Julianna took her hand from the table and covered her mouth.

"Permission to be excused?" Julianna said between quick breaths. "Please?"

The crow's feet at Aunt Maerie's eyes softened and her lips relaxed. "By all means, dear."

A brief twinge of guilt twisted into a knot a few inches behind Julianna's naval. Aunt Maerie had spent a considerable amount of time arranging this dinner with Duke Martyn. Many other high ranking men from other noble families would also be there – on the chance that Duke Martyn did not take a fancy to Julianna. Then Julianna recalled a party not even two months ago. Duke Martyn's hand seemed unable to resist pinching the breasts and bottom of every girl, and even a few of the boys, who served him that night.

"Thank you." The words came out in a quick whisper as Julianna bolted from the table.

In her haste, she knocked her chair over. The crash startled one of the new servant girls, who dropped a tea set. Shards of white porcelain and hot tea sloshed across the floor as the girl danced away from the shattered tea pot and cups. Julianna gave neither the accident nor the gaping-mouthed servant any attention as she fled the room. Her maid followed behind her.

Just as Julianna had planned, one of the downstairs maids waited right outside the door. Just like the girl who had dropped the tea pot, this maid had only recently come to the estate in the past few months. Aunt Maerie hadn't had time to burn their faces into her memory yet, which made them perfect for helping Julianna avoid Martyn Collaen. The maid stood with a bowl of watery gruel that also contained just a bit of bile from inside a lamb's stomach.

"Are you sure, my lady?" the girl asked.

"Do it," Julianna said. The illusion of sickness had to be perfect.

The maid dumped the noxious mixture on Julianna's sitting dress and the floor in front of her. As the mixture soaked into the fabric, the girl squeaked and fled.

Julianna made vomiting noises. She had spent many parties, balls, and dinners listening to men vomit up their excess liquor. Sometimes, she'd even sought out opportunities to listen to this activity in order to imitate those noises. One never knew when one might need to invent an excuse not to attend an outing or an appointment. The maid shoved the bowl into a nearby plant just as Aunt Maerie followed Julianna out of the breakfast room.

Behind Julianna, Colette and Aunt Maerie came out of the sitting room.

"Aunt Maerie," Julianna said in her weakest voice. She gestured at the mess all over the front of her dress.

Aunt Maerie brought her hand up to cover her nose. She looked about, up and down the hall. "You! Girl!"

The maid who had helped Julianna hadn't quite gotten around the far corner. She squeaked even louder as she stopped and turned around. Julianna felt that she might actually vomit. Had Aunt Maerie seen?

Aunt Maerie waved at the mess on the floor. "Run to the kitchens, get some hot water, and clean this up."

The girl curtsied and hurried off. Julianna took a breath, not realizing she'd been holding it.

"Oh, Julianna," Aunt Maerie said, taking in the sight of Julianna. "Your favorite dress."

It wasn't Julianna's favorite. She hated the vile thing, though she had worn it more frequently than any other in the past month. Aunt Maerie had urged Julianna to add variety to her wardrobe, claiming that the dress did nothing to enhance Julianna's complexion or her beautiful eyes. Julianna had countered by reminding Aunt Maerie that no one besides her, Uncle Alyxandros, and the servants ever saw Julianna in the dress, so it didn't matter how unflattering it was.

Julianna made several gagging noises as if she were going to vomit again, and then started off toward her room. After five paces, she clutched at her stomach and leaned on the wall. She wanted to hear any words her aunt and her maid might exchange.

"After her, Colette," Aunt Maerie said. "Your mistress needs you."

"Shall she be needing me to bring her breakfast?" Colette asked.

Don't overdo it, Julianna thought, though she could see the image of Colette's slightly faraway look as the maid spoke with Countess Maerie Vivaen. Colette was a more practiced deceiver than most of the high ranking lords and ladies that frequented court. Most servants were. It was a requirement of their position.

"Can't you see she's ill," Aunt Maerie asked. "She needs washing and a bed, not food. See that she gets them."

Colette dropped into a curtsy. "Yes, Excellency."

Julianna thanked all the lesser gods and goddesses at once. Half of her ruses and deceptions would never have succeeded if Colette did not play the part of the simpleminded maid so well.

A moment later, Julianna felt Colette's soft but firm grip on her arm. Together, they headed toward Julianna's suite, stopping every ten to fifteen paces for Julianna to feign another attack of her unsettled stomach.

Once they rounded the first corner, their pace quickened. They hurried past servants who were packing the multitude of paintings, tapestries, and stone busts that populated the walls and corners of her aunt and uncle's summer home.

Summerrain, a small estate of forty-nine rooms, had been in Aunt Maerie's family for over a dozen generations. It harkened back to a time when barbaric men still tried to unseat each other from horseback using lances and other weapons without the least bit of finesse. Aunt Maerie had done her best to disguise the inner antiquity of the estate by having the floors carpeted and the walls covered by as much art as she could. One of the servants' houses had been converted into an artist's house. Throughout the late spring and summer, Julianna had been forced to sit for a painter or a sculptor at least once a week. Aunt Maerie seemed to believe that Summerrain's halls could only be brightened by cramming them with as many renditions of Julianna and Uncle Alyxandros as possible.

When Julianna reached her rooms, she attempted to wriggle her way out of the sitting dress. Normally, this would not have been a challenging task, but she had an appointment, and every moment from her departure from the breakfast table to leaving the estate had been painstakingly planned. In the practice sessions at taking this dress off in a hurry, Julianna had forgotten to account for the vile concoction that soiled it. Her schedule only included time to quickly wash her body, but not her hair.

"Mistress," Colette said. "You're taking too long."

"I know that," Julianna snapped.

She stopped her wrestling match with the dress and went over to the bride's chest at the foot of her bed. It had belonged to her mother, and unlike many of the bride's chests young ladies used these days, this one was made to come apart. Each side, the top, and both bottoms – there was a false bottom about seven inches above the true bottom – were made of forty-nine interlocking pieces of carved ivory.

Young ladies used these chests to store anything they felt they might need for their wedding. When a man wished to marry a girl, he would ask her to gift him with her bride's chest. She was honor bound to grant him that gift. However, she was not required to give him the chest intact. If a lady disassembled the chest before giving it to a man, he had seven days to reconstruct it. If he did, she was honor bound to marry him. If the man truly repulsed the girl, she could always keep one piece from each surface so that finishing the chest became impossible. When he returned the uncompleted chest, she could then choose to reveal the seven missing pieces or not. That was the first challenge a Komati man must pass in his quest to win a bride.

Julianna opened the chest. "Colette, get the knife."

A knife lay hidden deep in the chest just above the secret compartment.

Colette thrust her hands into the chest, drew out the knife, and handed it to Julianna. From tip to pommel, the weapon was just a hair longer than Julianna's forearm. For the most part, it was a nondescript weapon. The hilt was a dark brown wood that nearly matched the dark brown of the leather sheath. The blade had a blood groove the length of Julianna's middle finger on one side. Aside from that, and the reddish tint of the blade, the weapon's only distinctive feature was a single word etched into the blade opposite the blood groove.

Kostota.

Julianna didn't know what the word meant, but every time she looked at it, she felt that she should know. She'd once shown it to Uncle Alyxandros, and he had quietly suggested that she might want to keep the knife hidden away, or better yet, dispose of it entirely. Julianna could not do that. It was one of two things she'd received from her mother. The other was her eyes. Her deep, piercing gray eyes were extremely rare in girls born of Komati blood, and they were nearly nonexistent in girls from other lands. It was the first of Julianna's features that most men complimented, and in doing so, they earned the first coin of Julianna's contempt. Complimenting her eyes was far too easy.

The knife sliced through the material of the dress, and in a moment, Julianna was free without any damage done to her hair. She tossed the dress into the chamber pot.

"Burn that horrid thing," she told Colette.

"Of course, Julianna," Colette replied. Then she pinched her nose with one hand as she balanced a tray holding a bowl of water, soap, and a washing cloth in the other. "But I know how much you loved it. I'll fetch the seamstress to commission a new one that is exactly the same."

Colette had perfected her imitation of Aunt Maerie's nasal tone.

"Oh, but Aunty," Julianna said in a tone of exaggerated innocence. "I couldn't possibly wear a counterfeit of the original, no matter how perfect. It just wouldn't do."

They both laughed and then composed themselves. They had only a minute or two before Aunt Maerie came to check on Julianna. Julianna slid the knife back into its sheath as Colette began to untie the strings of Julianna's morning corset. The door opened sooner than expected. Julianna dropped her knife, kicked it under her bed, and hurried to the window.

As planned, just outside the window, there was a splash of the same concoction that Colette had spilled over Julianna's dress. From the acidic smell wafting up from that mess, it hadn't been but a few moments since one of the other conspiring servants had spilled it there. The stable boy must have been waiting for the sound of their voices. Julianna couldn't suppress a small smile.

"Oh, you poor thing," Aunt Maerie said from behind Julianna. She still spoke in that condescending tone. Julianna's smile faded, and she clenched and unclenched her fists several times to keep from turning around and strangling her aunt. "Duke Martyn will be so disappointed."

Julianna turned around. "I can go." She kept one hand on her stomach and the other near her mouth. "Give me a few moments to recover."

"And allow you to embarrass me, your uncle, and yourself by rushing from the feast table, or worse, vomiting all over the high table at the main course?"

Julianna noticed where Aunt Maerie had placed herself in that list. Whenever she spoke of more than one person, Aunt Maerie always listed them in order of their importance. Oddly enough, Aunt Maerie usually named herself first.

"You will stay," Aunt Maerie continued. "Your Uncle and I will still attend and make our apologies to His Grace, *Duke* Martyn Collaen, Lord of Storm's Landing and Autumnwind. Did I mention that he has a seat on the Komati's advisory council to Governor Salvatore?"

"Yes, Aunt." *Only about forty-nine times.*

"*And*, did you also…"

Julianna stopped listening to Aunt Maerie's praise of Duke Martyn. She waved Colette to get the water and soap.

Gods and goddesses, Julianna thought. *Please let her leave.*

Instead of leaving, Aunt Maerie sat on the edge of Julianna's bed, and her foot came down on Julianna's knife. The weapon clattered against the stone floor.

"What's that?" Aunt Maerie asked and leaned forward.

Julianna stared at Colette. If Aunt Maerie found the knife, Julianna might not only lose today's activities; she might well lose the knife.

"Night below us," Julianna groaned and went to the window.

"Julianna!" Aunt Maerie cried. There was only so much profanity that she would forgive, even considering Julianna's illness.

With her back shielding her, Julianna shoved her finger into her throat. She gagged, but nothing else happened. With Aunt Maerie this close, Julianna couldn't trust her imitations. She needed to truly vomit. She wiggled her finger around, tickling her throat until her sides tightened and the porridge she had eaten spilled onto window sill and the ground outside. Julianna had never expected to go to this much trouble for a man.

"With all due respect, Your Excellency," Colette said in a demur tone. "I must ask you to leave so that I may attend my mistress."

Aunt Maerie sputtered. Julianna stayed leaning out the window, envisioning Colette gently leading the Countess of Summerrain to the door. The door closed.

Julianna stood up. Colette turned over a small sandglass that counted two minutes. As the sand poured from the top of the glass into the bottom, Julianna shifted from foot to foot. It would be so much easier to just jump forward a few minutes, but she might need the power to help her get out of Summerrain unnoticed. While she bounced up and down next to the window, watching the sand move in agonizing slowness, Colette turned down the blankets on the bed in case Aunt Maerie returned to check on them. That rarely occurred, but it had happened often enough to warrant caution.

At last, the final sands slid into the bottom of the glass. Julianna crossed the space between her and the glass in two long strides. She tipped the glass over and spread her arms. She and Colette had practiced changing from one outfit to the other twice a day for the last fortnight. By the time the top of the glass was empty again, Julianna was in her favorite burgundy velvet and black silk riding dress. Every time she looked at it, Julianna thanked the gods that Uncle Alyx could deny her nothing. All she had to do was tilt her head down, hunch her shoulders up, and give him a faint half-smile. It had worked ever since she'd recovered from her sickness when she was fourteen.

Once the dress was on, Julianna turned the sandglass a third and final time. Colette attacked Julianna's hair with brush, comb and hairpins – long, needle-like things that many men called "maiden's defenders." Julianna's dark hair was so long and thick that she needed between four and six, depending on the style of the braid. That morning, just to ensure the intricate braid remained intact throughout the day, Colette used seven. By the time the glass had emptied again, two curling ringlets fell across each of Julianna's ears, framing her face perfectly; the rest of her hair had been woven into a dozen braids that were pulled back into a bun and cascaded down her back.

Dressed and groomed, all Julianna had to do now was navigate the halls of Summerrain and get to the stables without being discovered by her aunt and uncle. Normally, this might be a challenge, but Julianna had arranged the work schedules so that all the servants who loved her more than they did the count or countess were on duty at this time. They were prepared to delay Uncle Alyx or Aunt Maerie with any number of questions or minor emergencies that could not wait.

Julianna opened the door. Uncle Alex leaned on the wall opposite her room, reading his letter. He glanced up through his spectacles. Julianna shut the door, grabbed Colette, and shifted backward in time a few moments.

"Wet cloth," Julianna said as she jumped into the bed and pulled the blankets up to her chin.

Colette gathered a bowl and cloth from the table, wet the cloth, and spread it over Julianna's head to hide her hair.

A moment later, a knock sounded on Julianna's door.

"Come in." Julianna tried her best to sound fatigued.

Uncle Alyx came in, still wearing his spectacles. He looked around the room, scanning, and finally fixed his attention on Julianna. He walked over to her bed and yanked the covers off her. He stared at her over the rims of his spectacles. Colette shrank to the other side of the room.

"Not exactly what I would consider clothes for recovering from an illness," Uncle Alyx said at last. He pulled the cloth off her head, looked at her hair, and shook his head. "It seems as though you have an appointment."

Julianna sat up. Uncle Alyx offered his hand and helped her out of the bed.

"Please Uncle Alyx," she said. "Don't make me go. This is my last chance to have a real seven birthday. My friends have planned a picnic."

He fixed her with his most disapproving stare, the one where his cheeks tensed so much it made it look like his lips were pursing to kiss something. "You know your aunt will be furious when she finds out."

To counter the disapproving stare, Julianna hunched up her shoulders, and gave him her best smile. "She doesn't have to find out."

Uncle Alyx shook his head. "There are times when your aunt may be flighty and obtuse, but she is not stupid. She *will* find out, and she *will* suspect I've had some hand in this. We'll both suffer for it greatly."

"Please, Uncle Alyx."

"Will there be any young gentlemen at this picnic?"

Julianna chewed the inside of her right cheek. "Yes."

"Anyone I know?"

Julianna ground her right toe into the carpet. "Khellan Dubhan and perhaps a few of his friends."

"*Baron* Khellan Dubhan?"

Julianna nodded. Even the mention of Khellan's name caused her ears to warm and her stomach to churn a bit.

Uncle Alex crossed his arms, sucked in a deep breath, and let it out in a long sigh.

"Well, it is apparent that I cannot keep you from being rash and impulsive, but I know viscount Dubhan and his son. Fortunately, they are both rational, level-headed men. You may go."

Julianna threw her arms around Uncle Alyx and kissed him on the forehead and both cheeks. He sighed and rolled his eyes. She'd done that ever since she was thirteen and taller than he, and he'd always pretended that he didn't like it but she knew differently. Uncle Alyx did not allow anyone do something to him that he didn't like.

Julianna gestured for Colette to follow, and they fled the room, heading toward the stables.

"If your aunt asks," Uncle Alyx called after them, "I will deny knowing anything about this."

"I'm a grown woman," Julianna cried back. "She can't treat me like a child anymore."

Uncle Alyx's laughter trailed after the two young ladies. Julianna knew better. Aunt Maerie treated everyone like a child, everyone but important people at court who outranked her in the order of precedence. Well, now that *Duchess* Julianna Taraen was an adult in her own right, she did outrank *Countess* Maerie Vivaen. Once Julianna returned from her outing, she would have a conversation with Countess Vivaen on who was and was not worthy to marry a certain duchess of House Kolmonen.

With the exception of Uncle Alyx's surprise visit, the plan to get from her rooms to the stables worked perfectly, just as they had planned it. Julianna waved her hand in frustration at the servants who curtsied and bowed to her as she and Colette rushed by. Normally, Julianna wouldn't have dismissed this show of respect in such a flippant manner, but Uncle Alyx had disrupted her timetable by several minutes. While she could have gotten them back, Julianna didn't want to risk tiring herself out before even getting to the picnic. So they hurried, not quite at a jog, but close to it.

When she and Colette reached the stables, Julianna stopped short.

"What are you doing?" Julianna demanded.

The serving boy and two of the stable hands were passing around a bottle. It was a bottle of fine Aernacht whiskey. It had been Julianna's gift to the boy for his assistance.

At the sound of her voice, all three snapped to the perfect attentive stance all who served the nobility learned to master early in their careers of service. The servant boy tried his best to hide the bottle behind his back. Unfortunately, they had already consumed enough whiskey that maintaining that rigid posture proved impossible. Each of them swayed slightly side to side, and none of them could meet her gaze, finding anything to look at besides where Julianna stood.

"Do you think that just because the nobles of this house are away that you can spit in the face of your duty?"

"No, my lady," the three of them said together.

"Excuse me?"

Julianna walked to stand a single pace from them. Gods and goddesses, she needed to get on her horse and get on the road, but she could not let this pass. The three of them stiffened even more.

"No, Your Grace."

"Better."

Julianna fixed her attention on the young man she'd given the bottle as a gift. He glanced up at her for a moment, but looked away almost immediately. She imagined what it must be like for him, with her eyes, the ones noble men were so quick to compliment, focused on him. His feet shuffled for just a moment, and then he caught himself, standing stiff again. They remained like that, a pace away from each other, Julianna looking down at him, him looking down at his feet. Moments ticked away to over a minute.

At last he said, "Forgive me, Your Grace. I will not spoil your generosity ever again."

"Accepted," Julianna replied and moved away from him. "To your duties. You can get as drunk as you want when your time is your own."

The boy bowed deeply, all trace of drunkenness gone from his movements.

Julianna turned to the two stable hands. "Our horses had better be prepared."

"Yes, Your Grace," they said in unison, and started for the stable doors. "They are just outside, Your Grace."

"Stop," Julianna said.

The stable hands froze midstep. They faced Julianna and resumed the attentive servant stance.

"You are drunk. You will *not* handle my horse while you are drunk. See the stable master. Tell him I relieve you of your duty for today. You can double your post tomorrow."

They bowed, shuffling off toward the stairs that led to the stable master's apartment. "Yes, Your Grace. Thank you, Your Grace."

She watched them walk up the steps. Once they knocked on the door, Julianna allowed a satisfied smile to break the cool mask of her displeasure. She couldn't remain angry with them. Not today, when Khellan was waiting to meet her and her friends to give her a true seven birthday celebration.

Two horses waited outside, tacked and saddled, just as the stable hands had said. When they came into sight of the horses, Colette handed Julianna a green apple. Julianna's horse, Vendyr, liked all apples, but he liked pure green apples the best. It was the only kind he would eat completely, without spilling some chewed-up mulch onto the giver's palm.

"Vendyr," Julianna said, and smiled when her horse's ears perked up, one black and one white.

All the horses at the Summerrain estate were of the Saifreni from Heidenmarch, a protectorate on the southern coast of the Kingdom of the Sun, all of them pure black with lush manes and tails. Well, at least all the horses ridden and seen by Countess Maerie Vivaen and her guests. The working breeds were in another stable entirely. Julianna's gelding was the only exception, and how the countess hated that blemish on her perfect collection. Vendyr was a rare -blood of Saifreni and Nibara, a breed from the Lands of Endless Summer across the southern sea. This mixed breeding gave him a white star on his forehead, one white ear, white socks above his hooves, and white patches on his neck and rump. This breeding also gave him strength, speed, and almost tireless endurance, thus his name. Vendyr was the name of an ancient Komati hero who had outrun the Goddess of Wind, the only mortal to ever have done so.

Now, even though his ears perked and he did the slightest dance of curiosity, Vendyr did not turn to face Julianna. She'd taken too long. Vendyr hated waiting once he was tacked and saddled. She let out a sigh and rolled her eyes at everything that had thrown off her carefully planned schedule.

While her plans did not depend on Vendyr being good this morning, he certainly could make the day harder to enjoy. Normally, Julianna would not placate him. She would endure whatever nasty little games he decided to play with her in revenge for whatever little thing she had done to slight him. Today, she didn't have time to struggle for dominance, and she suspected her horse knew it. The only question was: would he behave himself for the rest of the day if she placated him now, or spend the rest of the day testing her every step of the way. Well, there was only one way to determine that.

Just short of stomping her feet, Julianna walked right up to Vendyr's face. She offered him the apple with one hand and scratched behind his ear with the other. Vendyr whickered as he sniffed the fruit. He took one tentative nibble. Less than a heartbeat later, his lips pulled the fruit from her palm. As he chewed, Vendyr shifted his hindquarters, offering his flank to Julianna so she could mount.

Colette snickered.

Julianna leaned to her left so she could see her maid sitting on her own horse, Onyx, a pure black Saifreni. Well, Onyx wasn't exactly Colette's horse. A simple lady's maid could not possibly afford a horse in the first place, much less the upkeep. However, pretenses and appearances must be maintained at all times, so when they went riding, Colette got to ride Julianna's other horse, Onyx. In reality, Colette and Onyx had just as strong a relationship as Julianna and Vendyr.

"Really?" Julianna asked. "You find humor in this?"

Without bothering to hide her smile, Colette replied, "Of course not, Your Grace. A lady's maid is well aware of her station, and knows to keep her personal emotions reigned in at all times."

"Bah."

Julianna turned back to Vendyr. She hadn't fallen for this trick in a handful of years, but that didn't stop Vendyr from continuing to play the game: *I'll just look like I'm a happy horse, and I'll let my mistress try to mount me, and when she's halfway up, I'll move; won't that be funny to see her in her pretty dress sprawled in the dust.*

"Look, you," Julianna said, stroking Vendyr under his chin. It was his favorite spot. His lips quivered ever so slightly. "Today is not the day for this. Please, will you be good?"

Julianna knew that Vendyr couldn't understand her words, or at least most of them, but she knew he understood the tone of her voice. And after seven years, they had formed a strong bond, almost as strong as the bond Julianna had with Colette. The only trouble was that Vendyr did not recognize the order of precedence nor respect Julianna's title in any way. No horse did, no matter how much the nobility wished it otherwise. Julianna's familiarity with Vendyr served to remind her that, in many ways, the order of precedence was an illusionary construct.

As she had hoped, the tone of her words seemed to soothe Vendyr. He lowered his head and licked his lips, a sign of submission.

"Thank you," Julianna said, rubbing her hands gently over his face.

A few moments later, she sat in her saddle, waiting to see if Vendyr was going to test her in some way. He turned his head slightly to the left to look at her, lowered his head, and licked his lips again. Good. Finally something was going right this morning.

"Ready?" Julianna asked Colette.

"I was on my horse and ready minutes ago," Colette replied. Then with a wry smile, she added, "Your Grace."

Julianna blinked at her maid three times, sighed, and blinked three more times. Without any further response, Julianna kicked her heels gently into Vendyr's flanks and started off down the long drive that led to the road outside of the Summerrain Estate. By the time she reached that road, Colette rode next to her. They each urged their horses into a canter in order to make up for lost time. True, her friends would wait. After all, it was Julianna's day, but she didn't need to keep them waiting overly long.

As she left the hard task of escaping Summerrain and the last few moments of Aunt Maerie's dominance over her life behind, Julianna drew in a deep breath. She loved the dusty scent the drying leaves gave the autumn air. Now, barring intervention from some divine or infernal power, this was going to be the greatest day of Julianna's life.

TWO

Just as she had seven, fourteen, and twenty-one years ago, Yrgaeshkil stood and watched events unfold. This time she observed from a window on Summerrain's fifth floor. Few people even realized the room was here. She'd protected it through well-placed lies at corners and intersections all across the fifth floor so that even if someone managed to remember that this room existed they wouldn't be able to reach it unless they knew how to navigate the one true path of travel she'd left open.

Thankfully, she didn't have to wear the form of her detestable children, the one her husband had created for her. Today she was young, her body aged to about twenty-five years, sculpted to the height of male desire, full breasts, ample hips. Long, dark hair hung freely down her back. She reveled in the moment, as much as she could with so much weight on the outcome of the day.

Julianna rode away, down the long gravel drive that stretched from the front of the manor to the gate. Two flower gardens – each a twin of the other down to every single flower – sat on each side of the drive. This meticulous interest in the perfection of both gardens was one of several Lies Yrgaeshkil had placed on Maerie Vivaen within moments of Julianna joining this household after the debacle fourteen years ago.

"That was close," Kavala said.

Again, the scarred-faced man stood next to Yrgaeshkil. She hated how much she needed him. At least, for now. When the time came, she would rid the world of the nuisance of his presence.

"What was?" Yrgaeshkil asked without turning to him.

The door to the room opened and Alyxandros Vivaen entered as Kavala spoke.

"Julianna actually managing to escape to attend this picnic with her friends. It seems only a matter of luck that she was able to bypass her aunt's wishes."

"Luck had nothing to do with it," Alyxandros said, as he joined them by the window. "This morning has been carefully orchestrated down to the last moment. Julianna is a capable young woman, clever, and good at commanding the loyalty of those under her, but she is not perfect. I had to step in and aid her a bit. After all, this is our last chance, isn't it?"

Yrgaeshkil noticed that the mortal did not bow or show any deference as he approached.

She turned to Alyxandros, and the mortal did not have the decency to look away. There was once a time when all creatures knew their place in the order of celestial precedence. Most still did, all save for these humans. Well, the time was coming when she would remind them of their place.

"She will continue to have birthdays by seven," Kavala said.

"But they won't be this birthday," Alyxandros replied. "This is the first birthday by seven Julianna has had since the blessing by thrice has been fulfilled. It must be today, or we will have to start again, and it probably won't be with a follower of Grandfather Shadow."

"Alyxandros." Yrgaeshkil turned the fullness of her gaze on him. E-ven though she detested herself for it, she allowed her face to blur, putting a bit of her husband's preferred form into her features, specifically, twin goat eyes. "If this fails, you will not be able to hide from me, not in any corner of any realm."

"Why do you threaten me?" Alyxandros asked. "My part is done."

Yrgaeshkil wanted to slap this smug mortal so hard his neck would spin around on his shoulders. She turned back to the window. She could still see Julianna and her servant far down the road leading away from the estate. If Yrgaeshkil didn't turn away from Alyxandros, she might well kill him and cast his soul down into the Dark Realm of the Godless Dead for her children to play with for all time.

"Don't look at me like that, goddess," Alyxandros said. "Julianna is headed for the picnic. I have sent messages to those that needed information. I have affected today's events as much as is in my power. If this plan fails now, the fault lies with Nae'Toran and the Brotherhood of the Night."

THREE

The greatest, tallest, oldest oak tree in Koma stood on a hill known as Kaeldyr's Rest, which rose from the earth where the borders of three estates met: Summerrain, Dawn's Breath, owned by the Dubhan family, and The Shadows Crossing, owned by Mandak. This is where Julianna and her friends gathered to celebrate her birthday by seven.

For every generation since well before the lands of Koma fell to the Kingdom of the Sun, the young lords and ladies of all three families had gathered under this tree. In each generation they believed they met here in secret. And, as with each generation before them, they grew to inherit the positions, lands, and responsibilities of their parents, aunts, and uncles. When they began to raise children of their own, these once-young lords and ladies began to learn the skill of selective memory loss concerning this giant oak. Alas, most of the attendants at Julianna's celebration would not have the opportunity to learn this skill, for the young duchess was no longer blessed thrice by seven or seven by thrice, and these her friends would suffer for the loss of that blessing.

Fallow fields stretched to the horizons to the east and south. A stream ran past the bottom of the hill, going from northeast to southwest. A mill, long unused, stood on the banks of the stream at the exact place apple orchards stretched west. Amongst all this, the hill rose into the sky, and at the hill's summit, the oak rose higher still, like an emperor lording over the surrounding land. This tree had been planted in honor of, and marked the burial cairn of, the first high priest of Grandfather Shadow, the first Emperor of the Seven Mountains, and the first Komati ever to be granted a word and raised to Saenthood by any god. This small bit of knowledge had been stamped out of common awareness by the Kingdom of the Sun in the last one hundred forty years they had ruled over the Komati, as they had stamped out much of the knowledge of who the Komati had been in times past; but small details, like knowing this place was named Kaeldyr's Rest, could not be forgotten.

As the sun set on the evening of Julianna's twenty-first birthday, a fire burned approximately thirty-five paces from the tree. It was the place where fires always burned when people gathered at this tree. That night, blankets had been spread out on the ground near the fire, along with baskets of food and dishes. Bottles of wine, ale, and Aernacht whiskey lay scattered across the blankets. The celebrants had been there most of the day, eating, talking, and dreaming of what their lives would be like when they inherited their various birthrights.

As the daylight faded, they separated into small groups and pairs, believing, as young men and women whether noble or common do, in the illusion that night and darkness gives privacy. They believed in that secrecy with almost the same unwavering conviction as they believed in their own immortality.

A little way down the hill, toward the direction of the mill, another two blankets were spread out for the servants. They ate as well, only they had just started as they had been serving their patrons earlier. Unlike those higher on the hill, the servants did not converse much and did not drink at all. Drinking addled the mind, and gatherings like this were when servants needed all their wits about them, for who knew what tasty bit of gossip they might pick up to share in the servant's quarters later, or perhaps even a secret or two to sell to a rival family.

And so sunset darkened into night, the fire crackled, the nobles paired off to further personal and familial agendas, and the servants watched the games unfold.

FOUR

Khellan leaned against the giant oak. The warmth of wine surrounded his head and stomach in a soft embrace, not drunk, not even really tipsy, just…warm – the perfect bit of warm for this time of day at this time of year.

He had always loved this place, and he loved it even more now that he knew its secret history. It was always best at this time of day, when it was not really day and not really night either, the border between both places, when everything in the entire world became shrouded in the shadows of mystery. He stood away from the others, looking at the Duchess

Julianna Taraen of House Kolmonen. Julianna and her friend Sophya Mandak stood by the fire, speaking in whispers. Every now and then, Julianna would glance over at him, and even in this growing darkness, Khellan could see her eyes clearly as if it were noon. Those eyes were the silvery-gray of Tsaitsu steel and seemed to pierce everything Julianna looked at.

She seemed to like him, or at least, she hadn't seemed repulsed by his scar. Their conversations had never been unpleasant. Khellan had had enough women blanch away from his face in the last year to know when a woman grew uncomfortable with the sight of his face. The closest Julianna had come to that was a startled blinking of surprise the first time she'd seen him after Grandfather Shadow had marked him with the scar. If anything, the scar had increased Julianna's interest in him. Well, maybe it had. On the other side of the coin, she just might be taking pity on a poor, disfigured freak of a man.

"I know what you're thinking," Jansyn Collaen said, coming up behind him.

Khellan didn't jump. He'd heard the footsteps crunching in the twigs.

Jansyn continued, "You've been thinking it since the Mandaks' midsummer ball."

"And how would you know what I'm thinking?" Khellan asked.

"Let's see. Well, first, you're here pining away for her, admiring from afar, as you always do, and second, your mouth breaks out into that stupid, lopsided, asinine grin every time anyone mentions the name, Duchess Julianna Taraen." Jansyn leaned forward and spoke almost directly into Khellan's ear as he elongated Julianna's name, stressing her title.

Khellan's mouth betrayed him, the edges curving upward, making him feel, and no doubt look, like an idiot. Julianna just happened to look over at him at that moment. She smiled politely, or perhaps it was pityingly, and she and Sophya put their heads even closer together, whispering furiously.

Khellan elbowed Jansyn in the side. That helped him rein in his betraying mouth.

"I love you like my own brother," Jansyn said. "And at one point I would have wished the very best of luck to you in this. Not only is she among the most beautiful women in all Komati precedence, she's higher than you have any right to dare for. But you're not just some ambitious lordling now. How many men who have borne your scar have ever died old, in a bed?"

Khellan glanced over to the blankets, but not to Julianna. His gaze flitted over to where Carmine and Nicco flirted with Perrine and Sylvie.

The half-bloods might be cousins on their mother's side to Sophya, but their father was a High Blood of House D'Mario of the Kingdom of the Sun. While they were friends and had grown up together, that friendship might not last long if certain secrets were revealed. Carmine, especially, was an ambitious man, and friendship was the first casualty of such men. Khellan doubted the rest of his friends realized this about Carmine, and Khellan understood that he might not be giving his friend due credit because Carmine's loyalty hadn't actually been tested yet, but Khellan didn't have the luxury of thinking as just himself anymore. Not since receiving the scar.

Both Carmine and Nicco seemed to be focused entirely of the ladies. Perrine, the older sister, seemed to be enjoying the attention, but Sylvie rolled her eyes every time Nicco spoke. That didn't matter. Khellan just wanted to make sure their attention was focused on anything besides Jansyn and this conversation.

"Only one Lord Morigahn has ever died of old age," Khellan responded. They currently stood on that man's burial ground.

"One." Jansyn placed his hand on Khellan's shoulder and gave a squeeze. "Of all the men over all the centuries that Grandfather Shadow has blessed with the mark, he only deemed the first of them worthy to be surrounded by friends and family when the end came. I think you destined for great things, but Kaeldyr the Gray you are not. The only future you can give her is a widow's blacks."

"I know all that," Khellan said, "and I know my duty and responsibility as a Komati lord and the Lord Morigahn."

"Just remember that every marriage involving the Lord Morigahn has ended poorly, at best."

Khellan looked at his friend. Pity showed in Jansyn's half smile and the way he couldn't quite meet Khellan's eyes. Khellan laughed. It was an honest laugh from just below his navel.

Jansyn blinked in surprise and stepped back. He cocked his head to the side and pursed his lips. "I'm trying to figure out why you're laughing. I don't recall saying anything amusing."

"I'm just embracing my role as Grandfather Shadow's high priest," Khellan said. "This evening I am opening myself to the duality of Knowledge and Illusion. Between the discrepancy of my station in comparison to hers and that she does not follow the old ways in the least, I know, deep in my heart, I know that she and I cannot be together, especially if your grandfather is correct and we will fight for our freedom within my lifetime. However, I am allowing myself the illusion that tonight Duchess Julianna Taraen and Baron Khellan Dubhan might know love in a world without precedence or the conflict between our people and our conquerors."

Jansyn laughed as well. "Whatever helps to ease your conscience, *Morigahn'uljas*." Jansyn spoke the ancient form of Khellan's title with mock subservience. "Look. Here comes an opportunity to further your delusion. Oh, my apologies. I meant illusion."

Khellan looked back to where Julianna and Sophya were talking. Ingram, Khellan's best friend and Sophya's betrothed, was with the two ladies. He said something that made Julianna look away and sigh while Sophya hid a twittering laugh behind her hand. Thank all the gods and goddesses Julianna had never made a sound like that. Ingram offered his fiancé his hand. She took it, and he led her away from Julianna.

Julianna stood there for a moment, looking around, until her gaze fell on Khellan. She smiled and he felt his ears warming.

"Good luck," Jansyn said.

Khellan looked at his friend. "What do you mean?" But the insufferable man was walking away.

Khellan looked back at Julianna. She was walking toward him. The very edges of her mouth curved upward in a mysterious smile, or perhaps it was slightly mocking. She seemed to fancy him in return, but he'd never pressed the issue, going so far as to keep his flirting within very safe boundaries. He swallowed, mouth suddenly dry. Facing the challenges of the Lord Morigahn was easier than this. Still, if he was going to live in the world of Illusions tonight, perhaps he should cast off caution and embrace the boldness that the other Morigahnti would expect of him in the coming months and years.

FIVE

Sophya sat on the blanket furthest from the fire with Ingram Dashette's head in her lap. As they were actually betrothed, they could have a bit more privacy than the others. Well, as much privacy as they could get surrounded by friends and with that gaggle of servants watching from down the hill. To help give the illusion they were alone, Sophya had taken the pins out of her blond hair so that it could fall down, shielding them from the others as she looked into his green eyes, played with his hair, and pretended to believe all the lies he whispered up to her. She didn't mind the lies. She was one of the lucky few who actually loved the man her parents had chosen for her.

"Khellan is doomed," Sophya said, interrupting Ingram.

His eyes shifted away from her for the briefest moment. When he looked back at her, she saw an intensity in him that she'd never witnessed before. His face had grown hard, like a man preparing himself for a battle.

"What do you mean?" Ingram asked, though it seemed almost like a demand.

"Nothing serious," she replied. "Rest easy, my love. I just meant that Julianna is ready to give him her heart. She wants to marry him, and to be damned with precedence or standing or alliances. He might not be prepared for all that will come with that sudden, and unexpected, rise in station."

Ingram let out a long, slow breath, laughing softly at the end of it. The hardness seemed to leave him with that laugh, almost as if it had never been. She'd never seen this side of him, something that she would definitely have to learn about before they were married, but this was neither the time nor place to do so.

"I'm sure Khellan will be fine if that comes to pass," Ingram said. "He has cunning, wit, and bravery enough for any three princes."

"It still might not be enough to handle her, but it will be fun to watch."

Sophya pushed part of her hair out of the way. She could see Khellan leaning against the trunk of the great oak and Julianna standing near him, rocking slightly on her feet, swishing her riding dress back and forth.

"Oh no."

"What?" Ingram asked. He was also looking toward Julianna and Khellan.

"She's getting impatient or bored," Sophya said. "That's a dangerous place for her to go. She causes her aunt, the Countess Vivaen, so much trouble because the countess lets Julianna get bored. Unfortunately, Julianna drags both Perrine and me into trouble with her."

"Oh really?" Ingram asked, looking up at her. "And what kind of trouble does the Duchess Taraen get you into?"

Sophya smiled down at her fiancé and stroked his hair. "Nothing you need to worry about." He opened his mouth to protest or argue, but she placed her finger to his lips. "No. You will not get me to reveal this. They are Julianna's secrets mostly. Besides, what fun would it be to learn all of your wife's mysteries before the wedding?"

She leaned down and kissed him. When she lifted her head again, he was smiling with his eyes still closed. That was the easiest way to stop an argument with him. It might not work forever, but by the time it stopped working, they would be so far into their lives that they would only be fighting about serious things.

Sophya pushed a bit of her hair out of the way so she could watch Khellan and Julianna again. Her hair had fallen closed when she had kissed Ingram.

"This is interesting."

"What?"

"Look."

While Sophya and Ingram had been distracted from their friends by Ingram's curiosity, Julianna and Khellan had moved a bit. Now they each stood partially concealed by the oak. Julianna was on the south side of the massive tree trunk, Khellan on the north. The interesting thing was that their heads, Julianna's and Khellan's were completely hidden behind the oak. That wasn't too scandalous, as they couldn't possibly be doing anything from that far apart, but it did indicate a strong desire for secrecy.

"Well," Ingram said, "I am very interested to see how this little game plays out."

"Indeed," Sophya said, stroking his hair.

SIX

Jansyn walked over to where Raenard stood by the fire. Of all those present, save for the servants down the hill, Raenard was the only one among them who had not been gently born. In other words, he was common. That didn't matter overly much because Raenard was greater than any of these others.

"What do you make of all this?" Jansyn asked.

Raenard turned his head from side to side, making a slow sweep of the hill and everyone on it, ensuring that everyone else was occupied with their own conversations or otherwise distracted. Still, when he answered, Raenard kept his voice low. "I think the Lord Morigahn is a fool to be chasing this soft little duchess. I can't imagine how he was raised to be the first of us when it is so obvious that his faith and dedication to our god and order are matters of convenience. He should be busy planning to cast off the shackles that the Kingdom of the Sun has chained to the Komati people." Raenard glared over at where Carmine and Nicco D'Mario flirted with Perrine and Sylvie Raelle. "Starting with those two."

"Bah," Jansyn said. "Carmine and Nicco are harmless, and they are more Komati than not."

"You don't listen to them, then," Jansyn said. "It may appear that those two only have an interest in relieving those young ladies of their virtue, but there is much more to them than they present on the surface. Carmine is especially watchful. I wonder as to his presence here."

"He and Nicco are cousins of Sophya Mandak," Jansyn replied. "They are spending the summer with her family. She would have caused offense if she hadn't invited them."

Raenard snorted. "We should be taking every opportunity possible to give the High Blood offense. But I could go on and on without stopping about the idiocy of this particular outing."

"We've been given a great honor in protecting the Lord Morigahn," Jansyn said. "Especially one of common blood."

Raenard turned to face Jansyn and stepped forward so their noses were almost touching. His words came slow and quiet, yet the edge of anger in them was obvious. "My blood stopped being common the moment I completed weaving my *Galad'fana* and joined the ranks of faithful Morigahnti."

Jansyn tried to hold the commoner's gaze. He could not. After a few heartbeats Jansyn stepped back and looked away. This seemed to satisfy Raenard. He nodded and tugged at the scarf around his neck. "You would do well to remember that I've worn this longer than any of you."

They all wore the deep gray cloth that made them Morigahnti, though in different places so as not to be quite so obvious about it. Khellan also wore his like a scarf, which was all right, because it could be taken that Raenard was just attempting to emulate the nobleman's fashion. Ingram wore his as a sash around his waist. Bryce Anssi, who had already drunk himself to sleep on the other side of the fire, had his wrapped around his leg and hidden in his boot. Jansyn kept his wrapped around his arm.

As Jansyn thought about the cloth he'd spent the better part of his fourteenth year weaving, Grandfather Shadow's dominions whispered to him. No. *Whispered* wasn't the correct word. The tickling in the back of his mind was quiet but didn't come close to being actual words. The touch of them, the sound of them, and the desire they caused in him, urging him to speak them into existence, to pass through his lips as spoken language, as miracles, was a seduction unlike any other thing he'd ever known.

"I remember," Jansyn said. "And so do the others. This play that we are above you is only for the benefit of those around us who are not Morigahnti."

"Is it?"

Jansyn held his tongue. Nothing good could come of continuing down that path. There was a rift growing in the Morigahnti, between those born noble and those born common. He looked around at his fellow noble Morigahnti and sighed.

"Exactly," Raenard said, as if Jansyn's silence was all the confirmation he needed.

Deciding further discussion with the disgruntled commoner would only cause more problems than it would solve, Jansyn moved a bit away and picked up a bottle of wine. He didn't drink; he only desired it as means of escaping without causing too much offense.

Yes, the Morigahnti should work toward casting off the yoke of the Kingdom of the Sun, but there were so many wounds they needed to heal in their own ranks before they could even dream of defeating the Kingdom.

The sound of skin slapping skin echoed across the hilltop. It had come from up by the oak.

Jansyn spun around, ready to defend the Lord Morigahn.

"Julianna wait," Khellan said.

Julianna stormed toward the blankets and the fire. Khellan rubbed the side of his face and worked his jaw back and forth. Well, it didn't take too much work to guess what had happened. Perhaps this soft duchess did not fancy Khellan nearly as much as he had hoped.

"Someone fetch a pair of swords," Julianna said.

SEVEN

Julianna stared down the blade of her rapier at Baron Khellan Dubhan. The arrogant young lord had stolen a kiss without as much as a by-your-leave, never mind that she'd been secretly wanting that kiss for some time. She concentrated on keeping her left hand from touching her mouth, the small bit of wine made this more difficult than she had expected. His lips had been soft, strong, and inviting, and despite the way his smile made her forget to breathe, he would pay for his presumptuousness. She'd made other men bleed for less, but she hadn't welcomed any of their advances.

Khellan stood on the other side of the firelight, rapier held casually at his side. They'd built the fire up for them to see well enough for this duel. The heat of the blaze washed over Julianna as she continued to steady herself.

Khellan appeared disinterested, as if this was some chore that he'd rather finish so that he could move on to more interesting activities. She could just imagine what those interesting activities might be. The right side of his mouth curved upwards, causing his almost-healed scar, running from hairline to chin, to quiver. He'd worn that same smirk just before he had *pretended* to trip – he swore it was an *accident* – and caused their lips to meet. Whatever Khellan claimed, his brown eyes danced with mischief.

Just as her cousin Marcus had taught her, Julianna eliminated all distractions from her mind: her friends and the servants twittering and gasping about the impropriety of ladies dueling, Khellan's friends encouraging Julianna, likely because Khellan's defeat would provide them with months of ridicule, and most especially the wine swimming in her head. The smaller things went next: the aroma of roasting game hens from the picnic, the sound of horses whinnying at the bottom of the hill, and her ringlets, which the wind seemed determined to keep blowing into her face. The hair styling she felt had been so perfect before leaving Summerain became an annoyance she could not afford. She blew a ringlet aside, and this time the wind caught it just right and pulled it to the back of her head.

Khellan laughed. "Perhaps Your Grace would like a few moments to groom before we begin."

"His Lordship is too kind." She waved the tip of her rapier at his half-open shirt. He had removed his coat and vest to allow greater freedom of movement, yet had not removed the long gray scarf that always hung about his shoulders. "However, since His Lordship has decided not to properly dress, I'm sure our audience will forgive me a bit of loose hair."

"As you wish." Khellan gave a mocking bow.

Ingram Dashette, Khellan's closest friend, stepped between them. Ingram had also removed his coat, but had retained his vest and cravat. His bright green cravat caught the color of his eyes, which usually viewed the world as if he understood some fundamental jest the rest of the world could not fathom. However, just like any time he was involved in or watching a competition of any kind, those eyes appeared to be weighing and judging everything around him. Ingram could not tolerate injustice in any sort of competition, and so Julianna and Khellan had agreed that he was the one impartial enough to officiate the duel.

"This is only a minor duel," Ingram said. "Shall you honorably hold to first touch, or must I have your blades blunted?"

"You'd better not put a wine cork over the end of my blade," Khellan said, his smile growing. "It might get tipsy, and there's no telling what it might do then."

"I will trust that Baron Dubhan can handle a rapier with more skill than a razor," Julianna replied, "and will not mar my face the way he has his own." This met with a roar of laughter from his friends. "I will, of course, do my best not to give him a matching adornment on the other side of his face."

Ingram rolled his eyes. "Very well. Duchess Julianna Taraen of House Kolmonen, are you prepared?"

"I am." When Julianna spoke those words, her heart calmed. She *was* prepared.

"Baron Khellan Dubhan of House Kutonen, are you prepared?"

Khellan winked at her. "Always and for anything."

Again, another ploy to break her concentration. Again, it failed.

"Then turn toward your seconds," Ingram said, "and wait for my count."

Julianna lowered her blade. She turned away from Khellan to find her second smiling.

"It's likely you've beaten him already," Carmine whispered.

"I know," Julianna whispered in return. "They always underestimate me."

Of the men present, only Carmine and Nicco D'Mario had ever seen Julianna duel. Thus, Carmine knew that Julianna was more than capable of handling herself with a blade. All the ladies had, including the maids, and none of them were going to say anything and ruin the entertainment of watching Khellan's surprise when Julianna bested him. At least, that's what Julianna hoped would happen.

Carmine and his younger brother Nicco were the only men who could stand as Julianna's second without causing offense. True, they were Khellan's friends, but they were also cousins of Julianna's friend, Sophya Mandak. Because of that relation, either of them could have stood as Julianna's second without betraying Khellan's friendship. Carmine had offered, and Julianna had accepted.

"I will count off," Ingram said. "When I am finished, turn and come at your opponent. Be sure to hold off when I cry *yield*...One."

Julianna took in a deep breath, closed her eyes, and ignored everything except Ingram's steady count.

"Two, three..."

While her sword arm rested at her side, Julianna reached her free hand up to where her bosom rose from her dress and corset. In preparing for the picnic, she had had Colette push her breasts up a little more than usual, almost to the point of impropriety. Khellan had been unable to keep his gaze off her for more than a few moments at a time. Then a few moments ago, it had worked too well, when he'd taken liberties that he should not have.

"Four."

Her heart sped up at the memory of his lips on hers. Grinding her teeth, Julianna pushed her excitement aside.

"Five."

Julianna's fingers slipped into her corset between her breasts and caressed the hilt of her mother's knife.

"Six."

Sliding the knife free from its sheath, Julianna twisted her feet in the grass while keeping her hips and shoulders facing away from Khellan. She would need extra speed when she snapped around to face Khellan when Ingram finally called...

"Seven."

Julianna spun and lunged. It was a risk, but Julianna found most men never expected a woman to be so aggressive right from the start. Khellan was no different. He was still turning and barely brought his blade up in time to parry her full-arm extended lunge.

"What are you—?" Khellan sputtered while trying to retreat, but he found he couldn't move.

Julianna's right foot had come down on his, pinning it to the ground. They were so close, their bodies were almost touching. His breath blew against her cheek. Gods and goddesses, it felt good.

Khellan's eyes widened. The knife she held in her left hand rested against his inner thigh. She pushed the tip into him just enough to let him know it was there. His lips moved, trying to form words, but nothing came out.

Julianna leaned closer so that only two fingers separated their lips.

"Do you yield?" she asked.

Her words seemed to bring the life back into him. He smiled and leaned forward. Was he trying to kiss her again? She gave him a little poke with the knife, just as a reminder. Khellan sucked in a pained breath.

"You give me little choice," Khellan whispered through clenched teeth.

"And your apology?"

Khellan sighed. "I'm sorry for kissing you."

She jabbed him with the dagger again.

"What?"

His eyes went wide, as he looked into hers, searching for the answer she wanted. Good. It wouldn't do for him to have figured out everything about her already. Men needed a bit of mystery.

"I don't want you to be sorry for kissing me."

"Then what do you want me to apologize for?"

"For being so stupid to think you needed to steal what I would have given willingly."

Khellan's face tightened, and he gave her a look as if he were trying to solve a puzzle. He held that face for a few moments, then his eyes widened and he grinned.

Julianna kissed him. Let him know what it felt like to be taken by surprise. Khellan's astonishment was short-lived. Soon, he returned the kiss with an eagerness that bordered on hunger.

Julianna and Khellan dropped their swords and wrapped their arms around each other. However, she kept her knife, on the chance Khellan attempted too many liberties. Their friends called out many colorful jests and suggestions, but Julianna ignored them and melted into Khellan's arms. Damn propriety and family obligations. Now that she was a woman in her own right, she planned to live as she wished, even if that meant ignoring the rules and mores her aunt seemed intent on lacing her into tighter than a corset. Julianna wanted to marry this man. A man who kissed like this deserved to be a duke, even if it was only through marriage.

Julianna had no idea of how long she'd been exploring Khellan's lips with her own when one of the other girls said, maybe Sylvie, "Somebody's coming."

The faint sound of hoofbeats tickled Julianna's ears as she and Khellan ended their kiss. In the last light of dusk, Julianna saw riders coming from the south. They were still far away and rode as a chaotic mob, not the organized way nobles with their house guards would ride. She couldn't tell how many, but it was at least twenty, maybe more than thirty.

"Are they bandits?" Sophya asked, her quivering voice naming one of Julianna's fears.

"I don't think so," Carmine said. "What about you Khellan?"

Julianna glanced at Carmine. His tone had been too even, without a hint of concern. She glanced to Nicco. Carmine's younger brother wore the slightest smirk of satisfaction on his lips.

The hoofbeats pounded louder. Julianna looked back to the riders. They were close enough for her to make the count between thirty and fifty. She could just make out their black leather armor as well as the stark white skulls they wore as helmets. Her breath caught in her throat. These men were worse than bandits. The riders were the Brotherhood of the Night, followers of Old Uncle Night.

MOMENT OF GREATEST NEED

We must prepare for the greater gods' return. That event will likely spark off a Third War of the Gods. I fear it will be worse than the first two combined. We cannot allow either Grandfather Shadow or Old Uncle Night to be the first freed. To prevent this, we should endeavor to set the Morigahnti and the Brotherhood of the Night against each other. To this task, we must dedicate ourselves. To this end, we must not fail. – GrandMaster Myrs Byltaen to the Taekuri Council.

ONE

Khellan kicked his sword into his hand. He wanted to flee, to run to his horse and ride away as if Old Uncle Night were whispering in his ear. In all honesty, the god of death might very well be doing that. He took a brief moment to try and count the Nightbrothers riding toward them. Between the darkness of night and their numbers, it proved an impossible task, but he suspected around fifty of them.

Grandfather Shadow, Khellan prayed, *give me the strength to fight this battle.*

His logical mind knew that Grandfather Shadow was trapped somewhere, had been for centuries or more, and couldn't really help him. Khellan also knew that faith and religion itself was not rational, and he needed to be rational if he was going to live through this. He and his friends *could* live through this, at least he hoped most of them would.

"The mill!" Khellan yelled. "Everyone to the mill. We can make a stand there!"

His stomach revolted with the realization that he wasn't going to be able to save them all. He choked the bile down as he fled to the horses. Part of being the Lord Morigahn was about knowing that some of his people were going to die and that he was sometimes going to have to choose between good people living and good people dying. He just never imagined that he was going to have to start making those choices so soon.

"Ingram! Jansyn!" Khellan yelled. "Get down to the servants. Get them moving toward the mill and be prepared to hold that line. Raenard, you've the most experience out of all of us! Hold them here for seventy heartbeats, and then retreat to the mill if you can!

"Carmine and Nicco, try and get the ladies to safety."

"My brother and I are not your servants, Khellan," Carmine said. "We'll stay and fight."

"We should flee together," Julianna said.

Khellan felt a hand on his shoulder. He glanced back at her. Her skin had gone white. He wanted to give her a rational explanation, but there was no time. The Nightbrothers had already closed half the distance.

"Go, Julianna." Khellan jerked away from her. "Now!"

She blinked and looked as if he'd slapped her. She nodded and started down the hill.

Good. Better to have her hate him and live, than love him and get them both killed by staying.

"What about Bryce?" Ingram asked, as he and Jansyn headed down the hill toward the servants and horses

Khellan kicked Bryce in the shoulder. Bryce muttered something and vomited.

"He's in the Grandfather's hands now," Khellan answered, then looked at Raenard. Khellan knew exactly how Raenard and many other Morigahnti felt about him. "Hold them. Here. Seventy heartbeats." This command would most likely kill him.

Raenard nodded and turned to face the oncoming riders.

Khellan headed down the slope at a full run.

TWO

The ground shook with the power of the oncoming horses. Julianna spared Khellan a final glance before heading toward Perrine and Sylvie. Ingram gripped Sophya's wrist and was pulling her down the hill behind him, so she was at least headed in the right direction. The other two girls had run to the oak and huddled at the base of its trunk, as if it would protect them.

"Get up, damn you!" Julianna screamed over the thunder of hoofbeats, and inwardly sent up a prayer to Sister Wind to give them all speed. "To the horses!"

The goddess must have heard her. Sylvie stood and pulled on Perrine's arm. Perrine ignored it as she clutched the oak tree, seemingly paralyzed by fear. Tears threatened to well into Julianna's eyes, and a cold knot formed in her stomach when she realized that she would have to leave some behind. There was no time to hesitate; anyone who showed the slightest indecision would be a liability for the rest.

"Leave her!" Julianna yelled, barely hearing her words above the charging horses. "Sylvie, you only have time to save yourself!"

Sylvie looked from Julianna to Perrine. Tears rolled down Sylvie's face, but she nodded. They fled down the hill, leaving Perrine. At one point, Sylvie stumbled. Julianna almost stopped to help the girl but steeled herself against that. Anyone who didn't get to safety would be overrun, so Julianna followed close behind Sylvie.

Someone shouted up near the oak tree. Julianna couldn't understand the strange words, but his voice seemed enhanced by something. His voice sounded much like an Adept of a Greater God when the Adept spoke a miracle. She'd seen it happen twice. If an Adept of Old Uncle Night led the Nightbrothers, then perhaps Julianna should kill Colette now, and spare the maid the terror of possibly being captured. Julianna might have a chance at ransom, but surely Colette would be used as a brood mother.

The voice stopped speaking, and for the briefest moment the world seemed to hold its breath. The only sound came from the pounding hoof-beats. Then a wind rushed past Julianna, strong enough to force her back a step. She struggled against it. A moment later, Sylvie fell forward, sprawling to the ground. Then the wind vanished, and without the resist-ance, Julianna stumbled to her hands and knees. The ground scraped her palms, and the impact jarred her elbows and shoulders.

Unable to resist, Julianna looked back the way she'd come. The wind seemed to grow in strength as it went, flattening the grass and picking up dirt, twigs, and leaves; she could see them all swirling and spinning in the moonlight. When the wind reached the tree, it seemed to split around Raenard and the tree, leaving them unharmed. The Nightbrothers – the front line of them had just crested the hill – did not fare so well. Horses reeled in the force of that gale and men flew into the air.

Blinking her surprise, Julianna turned and scrambled to Sylvie to help the younger girl get to her feet.

With power like that to help them, perhaps this wasn't as hopeless as she'd first imagined.

"What happened?" Sylvie asked when Julianna lifted her by the shoulders.

"A miracle, I think. Best not to waste it."

The two girls got to their feet and dashed down the hill again.

Khellan was right. Getting to the mill was likely the only hope they had to survive, especially if somehow they had the power of miracle. Julianna would worry about the questions about the crime of it later. Uncle Alyx knew where she'd gone, and as it got later and later he would eventually come looking. Julianna could only pray to Sister Wind to allow them to live that long, but could she even hope for the lesser goddess to withstand the zeal of all these followers of one of the Greater Gods?

All these thoughts surged through Julianna's mind as she raced down the hill. Halfway to the servants, Sylvie sped past her. Julianna offered a quick prayer of thanks that the girl had not fallen when she had stumbled.

Several of the servants had fled, but most stood around, wide-eyed, mouths agape, waiting to be told what to do. Why were so many nobles afraid to allow their servants to think?

Of the horses, Khellan's brick-colored gelding, a True Bred, Carmine's black Saifreni, and Vendyr were the only animals that remained even close to calm. Two horses had pulled free of the stakes tethering them to the ground, and they were galloping away. The others were stomping and pulling at their tethers. Khellan, Ingram, Carmine, and Nicco were yelling at the servants and trying to get some of the horses under control.

Julianna grabbed Colette.

"We'll both ride Vendyr!" Julianna shouted.

Colette nodded, and after a few steps hiked up her skirts, which helped her get her feet underneath her, and kept pace with Julianna.

When they reached Vendyr, Colette cupped her hands together and helped hoist Julianna onto the horse's back. Colette untied the tether and handed it to Julianna. Julianna gripped Vendyr's flanks with her legs and pulled Colette up behind her. It would be tricky without a saddle, especially at the speed they'd require, but better to fall running than to just wait for the Nightbrothers to overtake them.

Julianna wheeled Vendyr around toward the mill. Up the hill, she saw Perrine just starting to flee as the Brotherhood of the Night came over the top of the rise. Raenard was lost underneath their numbers. She watched with her throat tight and stomach clenching into knots as their horses trampled Bryce into the ground. Perrine vanished with a scream a few moments later.

To Julianna's left, Carmine was pulling Sylvie into the saddle behind him. Nicco was already riding toward the mill, trailing behind Jansyn, who was riding double with Ingram. Khellan rode over to Julianna.

"We can't save them," Khellan said. "We can only hope to save ourselves."

Julianna nodded and drove her heels into Vendyr's flanks. They raced toward the mill.

THREE

The door slammed shut behind Khellan as he followed Julianna and her servant into the mill. Jansyn slammed the bar into place.

The mill was lit by several lanterns which had been hooded earlier to keep secret the Morigahnti hiding inside. Khellan never went anywhere alone anymore, not since becoming the Lord Morigahn.

The situation inside was worse than he'd hoped but not as bad as he'd feared. Carmine and Nicco stood shoulder to shoulder in the far corner, swords drawn. Four of Khellan's followers who had been hiding in the mill held weapons pointed at Carmine and Nicco, two of which were firearms. Maerik held a two-shot pistol, which looked huge against his tiny frame, but he was the best shot Khellan had ever seen. Off to the side, Saeryn held a scattergun at her hip. From her angle, she could catch both Carmine and Nicco in the same blast.

Sylvie and the few servants who had managed to make it down here were huddled together in the far corner.

"What is the meaning of this, Baron Dubhan?" Nicco demanded. "Are you also a traitor to the Sun Throne?"

Khellan sighed. Well, now he knew where Carmine's loyalties truly lay. Even still, Khellan had so wanted the mutual threat of the Brotherhood of the Knight to overcome that ingrained animosity.

"Ingram, keep an eye on the Nightbrothers," Khellan said, then he turned his attention to Carmine. "Put your weapons down. Maerik. Saeryn. You should both have your firearms pointed at the Nightbrothers, not at my friends."

Maerik and Saeryn glanced at each other. Khellan offered a silent prayer, hoping that they wouldn't force him to order them to stand down. After a moment, they went to stand at a window. The other two Morigahnti, whom Khellan didn't know, lowered their swords. Khellan stepped between them.

"Carmine. Nicco. Can we please talk about politics and who is betraying who once we live through the night?"

Nicco opened his mouth, but Ingram cut him off.

"They're at the servants," Ingram said. "They've stopped."

"They'll be killing the servants, Carmine," Khellan said. "Building strength to attack. We can kill the two of you now, leaving us without two able-bodied fighters when they get here, or we can fight together, and some of us might live. If we don't, then the gods can sort it out with us when we meet them."

"But you're Morigahnti," Carmine said.

Next to Khellan, Julianna gasped. He'd hoped that if she ever found out, that it would be under much different circumstances. Ah, well. He'd actually hoped Carmine and Nicco never found out, either. He liked them and didn't want to have to kill them, but he'd have to if either of them survived. Yet another unpleasant choice he'd make as the Lord Morigahn.

"Yes," Ingram said. "And so is your uncle."

Both of the D'Mario brothers blinked in surprise at that. The tips of their swords lowered, just a bit, but it meant they might be ready to shift their thinking.

"Is this true?" Carmine asked.

Khellan let nothing in his face betray Ingram's lie. "You'll never know if you force us to kill you."

Carmine and Nicco leaned toward each other and spoke in whispers. Nicco shook his head once. Carmine sighed, punched his younger brother in the shoulder, and pointed toward the hill. Nicco nodded. They both lowered their swords.

"Fine," Carmine said. "We'll revisit this discussion if we survive."

"Good," Khellan said, relieved. He didn't want to risk a fight in here, there was a chance that they might hurt or kill one of the Morigahnti before they fell. "Now, what do you know of the Brotherhood of the Night."

"Probably less than you," Carmine said. "You Morigahnti have been fighting them since before time was an idea. Nicco and I aren't high enough in Precedence to really concern ourselves with them, especially being half-bloods."

"They're coming," Maerik said, and fired his pistol. The *boom* of the gunshot echoed in the room, and acrid smoke crashed into Khellan's nose.

"See you after?" he asked Carmine.

"Indeed," Carmine said.

With that, Khellan went to the door and stood on one side. Ingram stood at the other, ready to slide the bar up and pull the door open. In a brief moment of eye contact, Khellan and Ingram shared all the joys and pains they had lived through as friends for nearly two decades. They also recognized that they were likely going to die.

FOUR

Carmine glanced at Nicco. They shared a sigh of relief. This last minute change in their plans had almost turned out very, very bad. They hadn't expected other Morigahnti to be waiting in the mill, and surviving that surprise had been a masterful display of guile. Well, no, Carmine knew deep down that luck was the only factor. Now that the tension lifted, Carmine and Nicco shared a smile and an almost imperceptible nod. The left side of Nicco's mouth curved slightly upward. Carmine bit his tongue to keep from smiling. If any of the Morigahnti suspected any sort of betrayal, they'd kill Carmine and Nicco without a second thought.

They had traveled a long and risky journey to make it to this moment, and at last he and Nicco would be able to prove their worth.

FIVE

Julianna crept to the window next to the woman with the strange gun. While Julianna had never seen a firearm, she'd heard stories. This one had to be a scattergun, longer than a pistol, but not as long as a rifle. Its wide barrel supposedly fired a mass of smaller pellets. The woman had the weapon braced on the windowsill with the hammer pulled back, the wick glowing ominously, waiting for the riders to get closer.

The woman, who was perhaps a few years older than Julianna, looked down. "You should—"

"Save your breath," Julianna said. "If you die, make sure you reload first."

The woman gave Julianna a grim smile and nodded.

"Morigahnti," Khellan said. "Veil."

All his friends, Ingram, Jansyn, and the ones that had been waiting in the mill, all took dark gray cloths and wrapped them around their heads, so that only their eyes were showing. Morigahnti. The ancient warrior heroes of Komati legends. Julianna pushed the thought out of her mind. She could try to comprehend that later, after she survived. If she survived.

The hoofbeats shook the mill. It was an old structure. Bits of stone and mortar shook loose. The riders came charging as one thunderous shadow in the moonlight. Julianna wondered why they were still charging. A cavalry charge didn't seem like it would do well against a solid building like this mill.

"Now," Khellan yelled.

Ingram moved the bar and pulled the door open. Khellan stepped through the opening.

"*Galad'thanya kuiva an eva ruth*!"

As he spoke the final word, Khellan brought his hands together. When his hands struck, thunder roared, the ground shook so hard Julianna nearly lost her footing, and some wave of force pushed outward from Khellan like a gale and pulled up leaves and dirt in its wake as it hurtled toward the Brotherhood of the Night.

The force hit the riders. The first row flew into the air and back into the second rank. Horses screamed in fear and pain. Few, if any, of those animals would ride away. Most of the men fared no better; however, some rose and drew curved short swords.

At that point, the riders who had not been caught in what Khellan had just done – a miracle, it had to be a miracle, a miracle from one of the five greater gods – dismounted and spread out. Behind those men, Julianna saw smaller groups of shadows approaching. These groups, four or five, stood taller than the men now afoot, and Julianna could barely make out black horses and black hooded cloaks in the moonlight.

"Attack!"

Screaming, the Nightbrothers who had recovered charged. Khellan stood his ground in the doorway. Here and there among the oncoming charge – Julianna could now clearly see their pale skull helmets – some of the Nightbrothers stopped and aimed crossbows at Khellan. Julianna almost shouted a warning, but Jansyn spoke first.

"*Vaejaro'tuletti suojo tass talo*!"

A wind grew and spun around the mill just as the Nightbrothers loosed their bolts. The wind knocked the bolts off course just enough so that Khellan need not fear being hit. How was it possible for her friends to have this kind of power? Why would any of the greater gods grant a Komati the power to speak miracles?

Yelling and screaming, the Nightbrothers came on, a mass of black-bodied, white-faced madmen. Khellan stepped back into the mill.

Gunfire rang out at the window. Julianna looked out the window to see Nightbrothers pitch forward, their leather armor offering little defense against the scattergun. She'd heard about the devastating weapons in whispers, but never thought to see one of those weapons stop three men short.

Khellan started to yell, "*Galad kranu—*" but his words ended in a wet cough.

Julianna looked to him. He was on one knee, blood bubbling up in his mouth. Carmine and Nicco had thrust their swords into his back.

"No!" Julianna shrieked as she reached for the past, grasping at it as if she were drowning.

She only needed a few moments, half a minute would be enough. She willed herself to that time when Khellan was still unharmed and opening his mouth to speak. When she was perhaps four paces from Carmine and Nicco, just as they turned toward Khellan, Julianna slowed, as if the air had become partially solid. Julianna fought against it, struggled to keep moving, but just as she reached the D'Mario brothers, the world held her trapped in place. Very shortly after she had begun to experiment with this strange ability, Julianna learned that some things could not be changed.

Julianna fought to move faster, even though she knew the effort was futile. She watched, helpless, as Carmine and Nicco stabbed Khellan from behind. Khellan coughed up blood again, and dropped to his knee.

Two Nightbrothers rushed in the door. Ingram killed one with a quick thrust of his blade. The second jumped at him, and they both sprawled to the floor. More Nightbrothers came in. With that breach in their defense, it was only a matter of time before they were overrun. But that didn't mean Julianna couldn't make one of the D'Mario brothers bleed.

Changing her intent, Julianna fixed her eyes on Nicco. Hoping and praying, Julianna reached for the moment just after the brothers had attacked Khellan. She moved as though everything around her was stuck in molasses. As she stepped up behind Nicco, Julianna drew her mother's knife out of her corset.

Letting herself fall back into time with everyone else, Julianna grabbed a fistful of Nicco's hair with her free hand, yanked his head backward, and slammed her knife into his neck up to the hilt. A dark fountain of blood gushed out of the wound. Nicco's eyes and mouth opened wide in shocked surprise, and his sword clattered to the floor. Julianna yanked on Nicco and twisted her body so that she faced Carmine.

When the first bit of that bloody spray hit Carmine, he batted at it with his free hand, as if he was batting at an annoying fly. Then looking at his hand, his eyes and mouth opened in an expression almost exactly like Nicco's. Carmine turned, and with grim satisfaction, Julianna imagined him taking in the sight of Nicco clawing at the wound, the light fading from his younger brother's eyes.

Carmine howled.

In one fluid motion, Julianna pulled her blade free, let go of Nicco, and flipped the knife so that she held the blade between her thumb and first two fingers. Nicco slumped to the floor as she sent the knife flying at Carmine. He dodged easily, but Julianna had only intended the attack as a distraction. She used that moment to kick Nicco's rapier into her hand.

Carmine recovered from her ruse. His eyes burned with fury and hatred. Good, but that wasn't enough. Carmine needed to die knowing that he would never avenge his younger brother.

Julianna prepared to attack Carmine, every trick her cousin Marcus had ever taught her fixed in her mind, when Carmine yelled, "Don't kill her! We need her alive."

Julianna tried to leap aside but wasn't fast enough to avoid the blow that struck the side of her head. She dropped to her knees and fought against the darkness at the edge of her vision.

Blinking, she willed herself to stand and keep fighting. Someone grabbed her. She struggled, but another blow struck the back of her head. The shouting and ringing of sword on sword slowly faded. Despite her efforts to remain conscious, the dim light from the lanterns and candles that filled the mill faded.

SIX

The scattergun kicked in Saeryn's hands. The three Nightbrothers heading toward her window screamed and their armor tore open. She inwardly thanked them for wearing the obsolete armor. Her brother was a blacksmith, and so she used his metal shavings as ammunition only because it was better against the Brotherhood's armor.

Saeryn stepped away from the window. She ground her teeth together and drew on the dominions of Shadows, Storms, and Illusions through the cloth wrapped around her head. She took a deep breath and formed the words of the miracle in her mind, visualizing what she wished from the blessing of Grandfather Shadow. Once she had the miracle firmly in mind, Saeryn spoke.

"*Varjo ja tuli kierre ja sielha tahlha!*"

Fatigue washed over Saeryn as a cyclone of wind and semi-solid shadows erupted in the window next to her. A Nightbrother had been climbing through. The miracle caught him, already precariously balanced, and spun him around. His head struck the wall, knocking his skull-faced helmet askew on his head. Saeryn couldn't see his eyes, but she imagined them rolling up into his head as the whirlwind flung him to the floor at her feet.

Wasting no time, Saeryn drew the knife from her left boot and thrust it into the sliver of space between the helmet and shoulder. She didn't have to imagine the gurgle that came with his dying breaths.

"May your god embrace you," Saeryn said.

She left the knife in his throat; it would help contain the blood. The last thing she needed was to worry about slipping in a pool of blood while defending her post.

The miracle wouldn't last long, so Saeryn reloaded the scattergun as quickly as she could. She'd never taken to the sword well, nor the precision shooting of the pistols and long guns, nor had she the strength for speaking miracles over and over, but she was a scrapper. She'd been in no less than five skirmishes with Kingdom forces, and each time she'd survived on pure tenacity, earning her way onto the Lord Morigahn's honor guard.

When she had the weapon reloaded, Saeryn released the miracle and got ready to repel even more Nightbrothers. One was already trying to climb through the window. Their eyes met. Well, she looked into the gaping black circles of his helmet. He froze momentarily. Shooting him would be a wasted shoot. She spun her weapon and slammed the butt of the gun into his throat. His neck made a satisfying *crunch*. He dropped his sword, and his hands beat on the window sill. Saeryn pulled her gun back and pummeled the Nightbrother's head twice. The white leather crumpled with the second blow, and the man dropped. He started falling backward, but Saeryn grabbed his shoulder and pulled him back inside so that he slumped across the window sill, making it that much harder for others to climb in.

Four more Nightbrothers stood behind him, waiting their turn to follow their comrade. Saeryn fired. The scattergun roared. The Nightbrothers screamed and dropped. Bodies piling up outside the window would make footing more challenging. At this rate, the Morigahnti might survive long enough for help to arrive.

Saeryn was just about to pull back, to wait for the Nightbrothers to try coming through the window one by one, so she could kill them one by one, when a hand reached out and grabbed her wrist. The grip was a vice on her, stronger than anything she'd ever known.

She pulled back at first, but that only lasted about three or four heartbeats. Then the desire washed over her, spreading up her arm to her heart, her mind, and her loins. Oh, how she wanted that touch to spread over her, caressing her everywhere and forever.

"Come to me," a man said, stepping into view.

His eyes glowed. Saeryn's mind screamed to fight. Rationally, she knew this to be a Daemyn, and death would be the best she could hope for by going to him. She closed her eyes, reaching for any strength Grandfather Shadow could grant her. But Grandfather Shadow was so far away and had never actually spoken to her. This wonderful creature, with this touch that could never be anything but the purest bliss, was here and now. Her body needed that touch, so she did not resist.

"Yes," she replied and climbed awkwardly over the body slumped across the window sill.

SEVEN

Khellan looked down, staring dumbly at the two blades protruding from his chest. The blood seeping from those wounds had ruined his shirt and pants. He gasped for breath, and it was like trying to breathe under water. He would have screamed as the two swords slid out of him, but he didn't have the air.

He dropped to his knees, closed his eyes, tightened his stomach, and forced himself to cough. Bloody phlegm splattered onto the dirt in front of him. That allowed him enough air to force even more of the stuff out of his throat so that he could draw in enough breath to speak. He drew in a deep, watery breath, almost choked, but fought past it. With his chest near to bursting, Khellan struggled for the words he would need to keep fighting. He remembered a story about Saent Kaeldyr that one of the older Morigahnti had told at the last gathering.

Looking up, Khellan focused his attention on the first Nightbrother he saw. He drew on the Dominion of Balance, and spoke, "*Suoda var hano mina vama.*"

One of the Nightbrothers rushing into the mill doubled over as he took Khellan's wounds. Some of the other gods allowed for true healing. Grandfather Shadow did not, but injuries and health could be shared and transferred.

The change was immediate. Khellan's pain was gone, and he could breathe again. His muscles tightened with the ache that came from exhausttion, and he wanted nothing more than to lie down and sleep. But he couldn't. He had to keep fighting.

Some instinct made Khellan roll forward and let the momentum of the roll bring him to his feet. He came up next to Ingram in time to parry an attack aimed at the back of his friend's head.

Khellan pointed at the Nightbrother and drew on Shadows and Vengeance. "*Tuska!*"

A blast of dark energy flew from Khellan's outstretched finger and hit the Nightbrother's sword hand. The hand flowered outward in a blossom of bright crimson.

The veil around Khellan's head tingled with the Dominion of Storms as Ingram spoke, "*Mina kehia turvata*!" He emphasized the miracle by making a sweeping gesture with his rapier. At Ingram's command, a wind with more force than a hurricane caught two Nightbrother, lifted them off their feet, and slammed them into the far wall with a sickening crunch of bones.

Khellan ducked under an attack and picked up a short sword in his free hand. He felt defiled using the weapon of an enemy, but he could regain his principles once he survived. For now, he needed to recall Grandfather Shadow's Sixth Law: *Morigahnti are born to fight and conquer.* He parried an attack with the short sword and counterattacked by thrusting his rapier into an opening in the armpit of the armor. Khellan twisted the rapier, and blood gushed out of the artery leading from the Nightbrother's heart to his arm.

Three of the Morigahnti were still up: Khellan, Ingram, and Jansyn. The others were dead, though they had made the Nightbrothers pay dearly for their deaths. Corpses littered the floor, making footing risky.

"Fight to the rear," Khellan yelled.

If they had any hope of surviving, they had to get out of the mill and hope some of the horses might still be there.

He turned to see two Nightbrothers supporting Julianna's unconscious, perhaps dead, body between them. No, not dead, Khellan could see her trying to waken. Carmine D'Mario held a dagger at her throat. The weapon had a long and thin blade, sharp on both edges – an old Morigahnti style weapon. The blade was slick with blood. Nicco lay close to them; his head lay in a growing pool of his own blood.

"Stop!" Carmine yelled. "Nightbrothers, I command you to stop."

The Nightbrothers stood down and stepped out of reach of Khellan, Jansyn, and Ingram.

"Throw down your arms and *Galad'fana*," Carmine said, "or she dies."

To emphasize this point, one of the Nightbrothers holding Julianna pulled her head back, exposing her neck. Carmine placed the blade against Julianna's skin.

Khellan's arms shook and his lips pulled away from his clenched teeth in a feral snarl. His chest heaved, though he didn't know whether it was in rage or exhaustion. Had he been a normal man, without the power of miracles, Khellan might have complied with Carmine's demand. Instead, Khellan dropped the short sword in his left hand and raised three fingers.

"*Tuska*!"

Three dark bolts flew out. Two struck the Nightbrothers. They pitched backward, faces evaporating into red mist. The third bolt flew at Carmine.

Someone stepped between Khellan and Carmine, and the bolt struck this interloper's outstretched hand. Instead of exploding, the hand seemed to absorb the blast of dark energy. Khellan looked this man in the eyes, eyes which glowed yellow-green.

Khellan's shoulders slumped. He and his friends had no way to fight the power of a Daemyn. Khellan dropped his sword and unwrapped the *Galad'fana* from his head, not that it mattered. Daemyns and such otherworldly creatures were immune to the power of miracles. Behind him, Khellan heard Jansyn's and Ingram's swords clatter to the floor.

"Outside," Carmine said.

Khellan led the way, hoping that somehow he might be able to ransom for his life and the life of his two friends. He prayed to Grandfather Shadow that some semblance of the agreement remained intact, at least enough for some bargaining power.

Outside, the Brotherhood of the Night surrounded the mill. Their pale skull masks seemed to glow slightly in the moonlight. Even trapped as he was in this situation, Khellan couldn't help but think they all looked idiotically out of place, wearing the same antiquated armor that they had centuries ago, when men hacked at each other with broadswords and axes. He supposed they would still frighten peasants, and perhaps the tradetionalists of the Kingdom of the Sun, but Khellan noticed all the openings and gaps in their armor, perfect for a rapier thrust.

The crowd of men parted, and four riders came forward. These men caused Khellan even more concern. They wore the long, black mantles of Adepts of Old Uncle Night. Khellan scanned for the other two, the Adepts he couldn't see. With an attack this size, there should be six Night Adepts to correspond with Old Uncle Night's sacred number.

"Adept Carmine," one of the Adepts said. "Where is Adept Nicco?"

"The Uncle has embraced him," Carmine answered.

"And we will soon follow," the Adepts and Nightbrothers replied in unison.

Khellan glared at Carmine. Carmine returned the gaze with the tiniest smirk, as if to say, *now we know each other's secret.*

One of the Adepts nudged his horse forward. He was tall and had light-colored hair pulled back away from his face. While he wasn't what people might consider truly attractive, he carried himself in a way that drew the eye.

"Lord Morigahn," the Adept said, looking down on Khellan, "I bring greetings from the First Adept of Old Uncle Night. He regrets to inform you that the agreement between our two religions is dissolved."

Khellan slowly swept his gaze over the dead Nightbrothers and to where other Nightbrothers carried the bodies out of the mill, Morigahnti and Nightbrother alike, taking the corpses up the hill. Sylvie, Sophya, and Julianna's maid came next, bound with hands behind them. The three young women were placed in a line next to Saeryn.

"I'd noticed," Khellan replied. "The Morigahnti will not allow this attack to go unanswered."

The Adept shrugged and turned toward the Daemyn. "This is the only one we need to fulfill our bargain?" The Adept waved absently at Khellan.

"Yes," the Daemyn replied.

"Excellent," the Adept said. "Feed the other two to the hounds."

Khellan tensed to fight. Better to die fighting than to submit himself and his friends to the whims of the Brotherhood of the Night. Before he could move, Khellan felt someone step just behind him.

Khellan also heard a chorus of deep, rumbling growls behind him. He glanced back to see four creatures that had once been dogs being led from behind the mill. Their muscles rippled under their skin, as if the Daemyns inside were trying to rip free into the physical realm. Orange eyes that burned like embers in a fire stared at Ingram and Jansyn.

"Don't," the Daemyn said, low and quiet. "Fight, and the hounds will consume your soul, taking you out of the cycle of life, death, and rebirth. Submit, and you will know life again."

The Nightbrothers who held those foul creatures released them.

Khellan turned away and tried to ignore his friends' screams. He failed.

EIGHT

As soon as the Brotherhood of the Night attacked, Theordon Barristis, Morigahnti and man at arms to the Count Alyxandros Vivaen, had fled the mill. Theordon nearly killed his horse racing to reach the Summerrain manor house. As he galloped down the gravel drive toward the manor, Theordon thanked the gods and goddesses when he saw the count standing on the porch.

Thoerdon pulled on the reins and his horse slid to a halt a few paces from the steps. He half-leapt, half-fell out of the saddle, scrambled up the stairs, and managed as much of a bow as he could in his panic.

"My lord," Theordon said between gasps. "The Nightbrothers are attacking Julianna and her friends."

Theordon didn't like the smile Count Alyxandros gave him when he said, "I know."

"Then, my lord, we must go and save her."

"No."

That reply surprised Theordon so much that his jaw worked itself up and down. He didn't know whether or not to protest or to berate his master.

Theordon started, "But—?" His master thrust a knife under his chin.

A warmth spread down the front of him, wetting his shirt and waistcoat. He suddenly felt very sleepy.

"Julianna does not need to be rescued by us," Alyxandros said. "She can call for greater aid than any forty-nine mortals can give her."

NINE

A slap stung Julianna's cheek. The bitter taste of blood filled her mouth, and she forced her eyes open. Carmine stood one arm's reach away.

Julianna dropped her head into her hands and shook her shoulders as if she were weeping. Peeking out through her fingers she saw him glaring at her. She reached back, pulled two of the hairpins from her bun, and lunged for him. Carmine spun away from one, and before Julianna could strike with the second, two pairs of strong arms grabbed her. She fought against them, but could not break from their grip.

After a few moments of struggle, Julianna relaxed, hoping the men holding her would relax as well. They did not, so she took stock of her situation. To Julianna's right, Colette, Sophya, Sylvie, and some of the female servants were bound, gagged, and stripped down to their undergarments. Khellan's friends lay in a pile to her left, each one drenched in blood. Perrine's body lay with them, limbs bent in awkward angles from being trampled. Four hideous dog-like things sniffed at the bodies. One of the creatures tore a chunk out of Ingram's thigh and began to chew noisily.

Choking back tears and bile, Julianna closed her eyes.

Another slap caught her across the cheek.

Her eyes snapped open. Carmine replied to her glare with a smug smile. "Before I leave, I wanted you to know there are so many things worse than death."

Carmine grabbed her chin and turned her so that she looked around the oak, past where Khellan's friends lay.

Khellan sat on his horse, hands bound behind his back, blood soaking his shirt and pants. One end of the scarf he always wore was tied around his neck, the other to one of the lower branches. His eyes opened and he looked at Julianna. Even though she realized what they had planned, she couldn't bring herself to look away.

Carmine said, "Now."

One of the Nightbrothers slapped the horse's flank. The animal bolted. Khellan swung into open air, body convulsing. Tears streamed down Julianna's cheeks as she watched until Khellan's body stilled.

"Good-bye, Julianna." Carmine slapped her again. This time she did not feel it.

Carmine walked over to where a large group of the Nightbrothers sat on horses, mounted his horse, and started away, taking about a third of the Brothers with him. Two of the girls were tied together on the back of one of those horses, but through the tears, Julianna couldn't tell which two. Those strange dogs followed after.

Someone pushed Julianna into line with the remaining women: Sophya, the girl with the scattergun at the window, and two servants. Julianna closed her eyes and let her mind wander to other places and happier times: dancing with Khellan, practicing swordplay with her cousin, riding Vendyr fast enough to catch the wind.

Footsteps crunching in the late summer grass, walking up and down the line of women.

"This is a fine looking group you've gathered for me." The voice sounded familiar.

"Thank you," a second voice said. "I always do my best to please you."

"And you say they are all virgins?" the first voice asked.

"Of course," said the second. "All save for that one at the end. Carmine D'Mario told me he'd had the pleasure of deflowering her two months ago, though it appears his seed did not plant."

"Well enough. I think I'll..." The footsteps paused in front of Julianna. "Well, well. What have we here? I may have missed you the night your mother died, but not today."

Julianna's head snapped up at the mention of her mother.

Two men stood before her. One she recognized and one she didn't.

The familiar one wore the black mantle of an Adept of Old Uncle Night.

"I know you," Julianna said.

"Yes," the man said.

She had seen him once, fourteen years ago, and yet had somehow forgotten him completely until this moment. He was older now, his face wrinkled with age, but now that she remembered, she recognized him from when the Brotherhood of the Night had attacked and killed her family. He'd held one of the silver rods that had helped to trap her mother long enough for them to kill her. Until that moment, Julianna hadn't remembered that her mother even possessed the talent of jumping through time. There were so many things about her life before the fire that Julianna couldn't remember.

"You don't know me," the second man said, stepping in front of Julianna. "But I've been waiting to see you again."

He was naked, and his excitement and arousal were obvious, but his eyes were what caught her attention. His eyes glowed with a soft, yellow-green light. It was a Daemyn, an evil creature from the Dark Realm of the Godless Dead. The Brotherhood of the Night often summoned Daemyns to fill human women with their seed, creating half-breed children in order to sew chaos on the mortal realm.

"I will accept this one as the full payment," the Daemyn said. "You can do with the other girls what you wish."

Men cheered. The women screamed as the Brotherhood of the Night dragged them away. She heard horses riding away and cries of anguish fading into the distance.

Julianna fought against the arms holding her. Death would be a sweet release compared to this Daemyn spilling its seed into her and the horror of birthing its child. Two more men grabbed hold of her. No matter how she struggled, Julianna could not overcome the four men as they forced her to the ground. Once they pinned her down, the creature ripped at her clothes.

"I could make you enjoy this," it said, and lowered its full weight on top of her. "To want this more than you've wanted anything in all the world. More than that pretty lordling with his handsome scar." Its hot flesh made her feel as if thousands of ants were crawling across her skin. "But I'd rather have you struggle, to have you fight me, knowing that it doesn't matter. You will bear my child."

Julianna did fight him. She kicked and pulled against the men holding her down. The Daemyn was right; she could only resist so long. Eventually the Daemyn would breech her maidenhead. Tears streamed out of her eyes, and her thrashing transformed into convulsing sobs. After a few moments, even her sobs lost their power and became little more than twitches. How could any god have damned her to this horrible fate?

"That's right. You have no hope."

She lay back, closed her eyes and wished she could die. Her despair woke something she'd only been aware of deep in the night after waking from a nightmare. Those eyes that looked at her from the depths of her dreams appeared in the darkness. Strange words rang in her mind. She didn't comprehend the words, but she knew speaking them would bring help.

Julianna's eyes snapped open. She glared defiance at the Daemyn, and spoke the words waiting to escape her for twenty-one years.

"*Mina sasta.*"

Writing appeared in the air above her mouth. The script was complex, the letters resembling a spider web. Memories came flooding back into her, too many memories for her to sort through, but they were all from before the night of her seventh birthday. She remembered Mother and Father raising her to worship and love Grandfather Shadow, no matter what Kingdom laws dictated.

"You should flee," the Daemyn said. "All of you, before she can speak again."

"I think not," the Night Adept said. "We have a bargain. Do not try to trick me. I know the games your kind play."

"I only wish to be able to bargain with you again," the Daemyn replied.

Julianna glanced at the Adept. His eyes flicked back and forth between Julianna and the Daemyn. She also remembered the promise she had made that man fourteen years earlier, nearly fourteen years to the moment.

Father and Mother had taught her to keep her promises, so Julianna spoke more words, words that had been waiting in her soul since the moment of her birth.

"*Galad'Ysoysa! Mina sasta*!"

Again, words appeared above her in that same spidery writing. This time the words were bigger and glowed pale and gray in the night. Something hidden in the deep dark recesses of her heart emerged from the same place where the words had come from. A weight she had carried for her entire life lifted from her. The world seemed to shift sideways in a dizzying lurch. Julianna's head spun as if she had stood up too quickly.

"Too late," the Daemyn said, though it sounded more amused than afraid. "She's freed him."

"You there! Adept!" Julianna called.

The Night Adept who had helped kill her mother turned from the words fading from the air and looked at Julianna. She smiled.

"I told you, my father's god is going to eat your soul."

GRANDFATHER SHADOW

They will come again, the greater gods. This event begs one question: Will it be too late for man, or too early for the gods? – Attributed to the Blind Prophet

Grandfather Shadow has the smallest army in the Eternal War, but his children are the most feared. We quietly assist the followers of All Father Sun and Old Uncle Night to destroy each other, sometimes with a few carefully placed whispers, sometimes with a sudden ambush on the battlefield. As always, once our part is done, the children of Shadow return to hiding where we wait to strike again. – Introduction to *The Tome of Shadows,* by Kaeldyr the Gray

ONE

Few things ever surprised Grandfather Shadow.

He wasn't surprised when the Brotherhood of the Night killed Khellan. Men who took up the Lord Morigahn's title rarely died of old age. With Khellan's death, Grandfather Shadow should have returned to the Temple of Shadows. There he would await a man worthy enough to pass through the trials and earn the honor of becoming the next Lord Morigahn and be bound into that man's mind until he died as well. So it had been for the last thousand years since the King of Order had locked the greater gods away from this world.

However, Grandfather Shadow found himself overlooking the scene he'd just left. The stench of blood hung in the air. For a thousand years he had known only two senses: sight and sound. And, even those had been dimmed by his imprisonment. Not only had the world of scent returned to him, but he could feel again also, like the cloth cutting into his neck and the blood soaking his back.

Grandfather Shadow smiled. The reawakening of these sensations meant he was free.

Free.

How many times had that word filled his thoughts over the last millennium? At last, one of his followers possessed enough faith and spoke the words that freed him from languishing in the prison imposed by the King of Order. The words still echoed in his mind.

"*Galad'Ysoysa! Mina sasta*!"

Kicking his legs, Grandfather Shadow managed to get turned around. A crowd of the Brotherhood stood around four men pinning a woman to the ground. She was Duchess Julianna Taraen. Her clothes had been cut to shreds. Khellan had loved her. From watching her through the eyes of several Lords Morigahn, Grandfather Shadow knew Julianna was a mortal worthy of admiration.

Two men stood at Julianna's feet, arguing. One drew Grandfather Shadow's attention more than the other. Instead of a soul, Grandfather Shadow saw the swirling, chaotic essence of a Daemyn riding inside a dead husk.

The Daemyn looked up at Grandfather Shadow, and its eyes grew wide. It waved the other man to silence, faced the god directly, and gave a deep bow. "When this wench spoke your name, I thought I smelled change on the wind. I just didn't realize how much. Congratulations on your freedom."

"Do not play false pleasantries on me." Grandfather Shadow's voice boomed despite the cloth constricting his throat.

"Forgive me, Great One." The Daemyn prostrated itself before Grandfather Shadow. "Is there anything I can offer that will convince you to spare my existence?"

This show of cowardice was so typical of its kind. Daemyns were arrogant and cruel when they dealt from a position of strength, but resorted to false subservience whenever they had lost the upper hand.

"Doubtful, but it might be entertaining. Try."

The man who had been arguing with the Daemyn pushed his way past the creature, dragging Julianna by her hair. She struggled, until he put a knife to her throat. This calmed her, but the burning hatred remained in her eyes. The knife was an old Morigahnti weapon, long and thin, favored as a last resort weapon because it could be easily hidden in a sleeve or boot. Odd that this one had the reddish blade of Faerii steal.

The man wore the black mantle of a priest of Old Uncle Night. The mantle hung open. He was naked underneath, the weapon between his legs stood ready. It was likely that all of these men would have a turn at her once the Daemyn had planted its seed. Grandfather Shadow detected pieces of bone woven into the fabric of the man's mantle. These bones had been blessed to channel the divine energy of Old Uncle Night, making the priest an Adept, able to effect change in the world by speaking miracles through Old Uncle Night's divine language.

Grandfather Shadow ignored the Adept and looked at Julianna. At twenty-one years old, she was barely a woman by Komati tradition. Her long brown hair was pulled into the Adept's fist, and her gray eyes looked up, pleading for help. Tears of hatred and rage rolled down her cheeks. Words written in his holy language of *Galad'laman* hung in the air above her head. How had she managed to speak a miracle of true faith?

Peering into her spirit, Grandfather Shadow could not find any faith that would have freed him.

"Lord Morigahn, we underestimated your faith, and that of your woman," the Adept said, drawing Grandfather Shadow's attention. "But will it save you from a blade through your heart?"

The Adept raised the dagger, preparing to strike Grandfather Shadow in the chest.

Julianna howled.

She twisted her head and sank her teeth into the Adept's naked thigh. He shrieked, dropped his dagger, and backhanded her across the face. She tore a chunk of flesh out of his leg as she sprawled to the ground. Once free, she snatched up his weapon. Leaping at her rapist, Julianna buried the blade deep in his side. Before anyone could react, she spun around and stabbed another man in the eye.

The Nightbrothers recovered from their shock and rushed Julianna. She slashed at them, but there were too many and the weapon too small to dissuade their thirst for vengeance.

Grandfather Shadow refused to allow them to harm his rescuer. With the smallest effort of will, he brought the Nightbrothers' shadows to life and commanded the shadows to flay their owners' skin from muscle and bone. Blood spilled on the ground, forming small ponds and streams. Agonized screams hit Grandfather Shadow's ears. The sound offended him, so he solidified the shadows in their mouths, gagging them.

As the Brothers died quietly, Grandfather Shadow turned back to the Daemyn.

"Nae'Toran'borlahisth, isn't it?"

"Yes, Great One," the Daemyn replied.

Upon speaking the Daemyn's name, full and true, the creature's subservience became a bit more honest.

"Have you thought of anything that might convince me to allow your worthless existence to continue? Keep in mind, I remember all the ill you have done my followers over the centuries."

"I can offer you two things," the Daemyn said. "If you agree to do me no harm until the sun rises again, I will tell you how this mortal called you from your prison, and I will never raise my hand against any true Morigahnti so long as you remain the Grandfather of Shadows."

"I accept," Grandfather Shadow said.

"Excellent," the Daemyn said, getting to its feet. "By ancient tradition the pact is made, binding our agreement."

Its subservient demeanor had vanished. The bargain had been struck far too easily. Well, it was too late for looking back. The bargain had been set, and could not be renegotiated.

"Tell me how this girl freed me," Grandfather Shadow commanded.

The Daemyn smiled, and its eyes glowed a deeper green. "Your first and most beloved follower, Saent Kaeldyr the Gray, placed his faith into this girl's soul the moment before her birth. To what end, I did not know until this moment. He was punished and cast into the Realm of the Godless Dead."

"Kaeldyr is gone?" Grandfather Shadow asked.

"Oh no." The Daemyn's eyes sparkled. "I still keep him as a play toy."

"Be gone before I decide to ignore our bargain," Grandfather Shadow snapped.

"You wouldn't break your word for fear of being placed back in your prison."

"I wouldn't?"

The Daemyn fled from the physical realm, and the body it had possessed crumbled to dust.

Standing alone, Grandfather Shadow regarded Julianna.

TWO

Julianna vomited as the Nightbrothers died. When nothing remained in her stomach, her sides ached as if she'd been beaten. She still felt polluted by the Daemyn's touch and wanted nothing more than to roll into a ball until the feeling subsided. In that moment, she vowed never to show weakness again.

She lifted her head to find the thing inside Khellan's body looking at her. She still held the knife in her hand, her mother's knife, keeping the blade between them as she struggled to her feet. Fighting dizziness that came from standing so quickly, she edged a few steps to her left. From there she could dive into a roll and come up with a sword in her hand. It was one of the Nightbrother's short swords, which she could not use as well as a rapier, but it was better than nothing.

"I will not harm you." The thing spoke with Khellan's voice, but not with his charm.

"Who are you, really?" Julianna demanded. Having a rational discussion with Khellan *after* she'd watched him die seemed dull compared to everything else she'd just witnessed.

"I am Khellan. I am a priest of a god forbidden by Kingdom law. My god granted me one final blessing to save you before I ascend to the celestial realms."

"Liar." Khellan's eyes danced with mischief. "Who are you?"

Khellan – even though Julianna knew it wasn't her love, she couldn't think of him in any other way – returned her questions with silence. His eyes bore into hers. She shifted under the weight of his gaze.

"Shadows lie to their enemies, not to each other," Khellan-who-was-not-Khellan said. "You are correct. You deserve more of an answer than that, if for no other reason than for your part in this. The man you loved was the Lord Morigahn."

"You're a madman," Julianna said. "The Lord Morigahn is a legend."

She also knew that her own words were false. Memories long forgotten reminded her that her own father had been the Lord Morigahn before the Brotherhood of the Night had killed him. She was now repeating the lies the Kingdom spread to all Komati children in order to keep them good little subjects of the realm.

"I promised you the truth, and then you doubt me when I give it? I suppose showing you will be easier than trying to convince you."

In less than a heartbeat, faster than Julianna could react, Khellan was suddenly in front of her. He put his hand on her wrist and lowered her knife. His touch was gentle as a shadow's caress on a hot day, but behind it she felt the power and strength of a storm.

"Look into my eyes." Khellan's voice carried the weight of ages. Julianna obeyed. "I am Galad'Ysoysa, Grandfather Shadow, the true god of your people. Khellan was the Lord Morigahn. The Brotherhood of the Night killed him for this, just as they killed your mother."

"My mother?" Julianna's heart and stomach twisted together. "I remember."

"Yes. Both your parents followed the old ways of Koma. They worshipped me despite the laws of the Kingdom of the Sun. The Brotherhood executed your mother. However, it could have just as easily been Inquisitors of House Floraen. Ever since the Kingdom of the Sun conquered Koma, thousands of innocents have been killed merely for following the traditions I gave to your people long before the four Great Houses joined to form their Kingdom.

"But it doesn't have to be this way. Koma can be free. If you take Khellan's place and serve me as the Lord Morigahn, I will teach you to speak with the power of storms, to pierce the secrets of the world, and act as the hand of vengeance."

"Vengeance?"

She remembered that Vengeance was one of Grandfather Shadow's seven dominions. She glanced down at the knife in her hand and the word she saw there, covered in the drying blood of a betrayer. *Kostota.* Revenge. But in *Galad'laman* it had so many subtleties based on context. That was the trick with what little she recalled of Grandfather Shadow's language – so many of the words relied on context for definition.

Julianna looked around. Death surrounded her: the skinned bodies of the Brotherhood of the night, Perrine and her twisted limbs, and Khellan's friends, slaughtered just for daring to follow the traditions of their people. She recalled Carmine and Nicco stabbing Khellan from behind, herself as she took Nicco's life, remembered the feel of his blood washing over her hands as the light faded from his eyes. How good that had felt.

Grandfather Shadow came and placed his hands on her shoulders. She felt the raw power in his grip. It didn't hurt, but she had no doubt that he could crush her shoulders into pulp if that had been his desire. The god turned her so that she looked at Nicco. She looked at her hands, still covered with Nicco's blood and remembered the satisfaction she felt at ending his life.

"Serve me," Grandfather Shadow whispered into her ear, "and I will give you the power of revenge over any who have wronged you."

"Anyone?"

"Anyone," Grandfather Shadow replied. "I will lead you to seek vengeance for yourself, your friends, Khellan, and your mother."

"My mother? How is that possible?"

"I control many Dominions, second in number only to All Father Sun. None of your enemies shall escape you. Not even Carmine D'Mario."

More than anything else, Julianna wanted to kill Carmine D'Mario, but she knew she could not do it on her own. He was Kingdom High Blood, trafficked with Daemyns, and seemed to hold a position of some authority in the Brotherhood of the Night. To truly hunt him, she would need power comparable to that. Julianna yearned to see Carmine lying on his back, staring at the sky with the same blank expression as Nicco. Once she finished with that task, then she could seek out the men who had killed her mother.

In that moment, Julianna believed the truth of who Grandfather Shadow was.

Julianna faced Grandfather Shadow. "I accept."

"Excellent."

THREE

Grandfather Shadow passed a hand over Julianna's eyes and put her in that place halfway between the sleeping and waking worlds. He took the knife from Julianna's hand and examined it. The blade was made of Faerii steel, a rare weapon indeed.

"Where did you get this?" Grand Father Shadow asked.

Julianna took in a deep breath, and answered in a long, sleepy-sounding tone, "It was my mother's. I've had it since she died."

Excellent. Marking someone as the Lord Morigahn was always best with a weapon of deep personal significance. This weapon would do just nicely.

He placed the blade of Julianna's knife into the fire.

Being Faerii steel, it would take the weapon a long time to heat enough for Grandfather Shadow's needs.

Giving the weapon time to heat, Grandfather Shadow sent his perceptions across the world, searching for those who still had faith in him. At one time, everyone in this land had followed him and many could command miracles. Now, only a pitiful few of the Komati truly believed. Without the Greater Gods to direct human faith, it seemed that faith itself had become tainted. Mortal man had turned religion into something to fear and mourn when it should exalt their lives. Even at the worst of times, when besieged on all sides by the followers of all the other gods, the Komati had found joy in their relationship with Grandfather Shadow. Now even the faithful lived in fear of discovery by this Kingdom of the Sun, as it was called now.

So it seemed that he must again save his people. He looked at Julianna. Was she the proper choice to lead the Morigahnti to greatness again? Perhaps. The similarities between her and Kaeldyr were not lost on him. Many centuries before, a young man looking for help had accidentally discovered Grandfather Shadow. Julianna, needing help, had also called out to him. Both then and now, the Komati people needed Grandfather Shadow to guide them from underneath the yoke of oppression.

Grandfather recognized something in Julianna, a spark he hadn't seen since the day Kaeldyr had stumbled into that cave. Maybe it was a product of having Kaeldyr's faith bottled up inside her, but Grandfather Shadow didn't think so. Kaeldyr had been searching for something to latch onto and dove into the faith of Grandfather Shadow without looking back. Julianna would be different. She had once believed, as much as a child could believe, but had forgotten. Also, Grandfather Shadow saw something in this young woman he hadn't seen in any of his previous followers.

Julianna Taraen would be the first Lord Morigahn truly marked by the hand of Grandfather Shadow free of his prison in a thousand years. But first, she would need certain things, things that had been long forgotten by those who followed him.

Well, the blade would take time to heat. He could use that time to fetch those things Julianna would need to reunite the Morigahnti and the Komati people.

FOUR

Yrgaeshkil waited a few minutes after Grandfather Shadow left before she partially dropped the Lie that she'd used to conceal herself in the mill – except she maintained it for that scrying cauldron that someone was using to watching from some distance away. The goddess had been there most of the afternoon and all of the night, watching and waiting. She'd observed Alyxandros's servant running off, the fight between her husband's followers and the Morigahnti, and the events that had freed Grandfather Shadow from his prison. At last she could raise herself to her rightful station, though caution was still warranted.

As she walked out of the mill, Kavala stood there leaning against the outer wall.

"It went well?" he asked.

If she could have, Yrgaeshkil would have flayed the mortal's mind with Lie after Lie until nothing remained of him but a sniveling creature that could retain no sense of Truth at all. Unfortunately, no divine or infernal power could touch the man.

"Even better than I had hoped," Yrgaeshkil replied. "Grandfather Shadow has personally named a Lord Morigahn, and if my sources are correct, he will soon place a Saent in the world. Compared to that, what can the King of Order do to me for simply claiming what is rightfully mine by marriage?"

"Been playing with Stormseekers again?" Kavala asked.

Yrgaeshkil fingered the wolf-skin mantle she wore about her shoulders.

"The rest aren't going to be pleased by that."

She shrugged in response. "Considering that many of my children find them a delicacy, I hardly think one torture and murder will make things significantly worse."

"I suppose you're right," Kavala said. "As for the here and now, it seems the previous failures to draw the God of Shadows forth were not really failures at all." Kavala's voice held a smug tone that Yrgaeshkil did not like.

"Yes," Yrgaeshkil replied. "And, as the mortals say, it has taught me that patience is a worthy virtue. I will wait and watch for my proper time to strike. I'm sure that Grandfather Shadow will not be able to contain himself, especially considering that he is currently the only Greater Eldar free in any realm. He won't be able to resist meddling with his precious little Komati."

"Well, then," Kavala said. "I'm pleased that everything is working, if not according to the original schedule, at least to your benefit. If you will excuse me, I've been away from court almost long enough to be missed. Nae'Toran, always a pleasure."

As he spoke the words, Nae'Toran materialized in his true form, horns, bat's head, wings, and all. Yrgaeshkil turned away from Kavala before he vanished. She didn't understand how his strange powers worked without some form of divine blessing, but she did know that it churned something inside her as if she were a mortal creature with mortal frailties.

"What would you have me do now, Mother?" Nae'Toran asked.

To that, the Mother of Daemyns smiled. "Avail yourself to any Adept of Night that calls to you or wishes to bargain with a Daemyn. Sow chaos wherever you can, especially amongst the Morigahnti and Adepts of House Kaesiak."

"As you wish, Mother."

Nae'Toran vanished, and Yrgaeshkil walked up the hill to the multitude of corpses lying sprawled about the oak. Two of those corpses held particular interest for her – the two Morigahnti killed by the Daemyn hounds. She knelt down next to them and touched the one with pretty green eyes on the cheek. With his soul gone, not just ascended to the celestial realms but devoured by the Daemyn hounds and sent to the Realm of Godless Dead, his skin felt like moist leather. The Goddess of Lies took hold of the Morigahnti's chin and turned his face this way and that, memorizing his features. His soul would be wearing this same face in her husband's realm, and she wanted to find him. She meant to question his soul quite thoroughly about the current state of the Morigahnti, and she meant to take full advantage of his friendship with the most recent Lord Morigahn.

Yrgaeshkil looked over at Julianna and considered killing the girl, or better, giving her to Nae'Toran as a plaything. He could place her soul right next to Kaeldyr's. But no. That would not do. Grandfather Shadow would return soon, and if Yrgaeshkil guessed anything about the knife currently heating in the fire, she knew what that was about. If the God of Vengeance returned and found his new favorite pet missing, his wrath would be terrible. She would not risk that so soon.

The wind picked up. It carried a hint of divine power, a touch of heat and light that made her skin crawl. Yrgaeshkil cocked her head to the side and reached outward with her divine senses. Close by, she felt the blazing white power of All Father Sun – not enough to actually be the god, but enough for it to be one or more divine foci dedicated to the God of Truth and Light.

For a moment, she considered leaving, not in flight but out of caution. After a moment, she changed her mind, went to the oak, leaned against it, and wrapped herself in a Lie.

FIVE

Grandfather Shadow stepped back into the physical realm. Being in his proper body felt far better than being trapped in Khellan's corpse. He closed his eyes and took a deep breath, not because he needed to, but rather because he wanted to revel in any sensation he could.

The air was chilly without being cold, the kind of autumn air where a man could be comfortable in just a coat or a light cloak. The air smelled of pine and earth. The dull ever-constant roar of the wind through the pine needles was like a symphony to his ears. How he missed that sound. It had been too slight a sound to really perceive while trapped in the multitudes of Lords Morigahn over the centuries.

Opening his eyes, Grandfather Shadow exhaled.

A large wolf, larger than any natural animal could claim to be, sat on its haunches regarding the Greater Eldar. The beast was mostly black. White and gray peppered the wolf's muzzle, paws, ears, flanks, and tail. It had been completely black at one point in its life, but neither Grandfather Shadow, nor any other creature, save for another of the wolf's kind, could tell its age or where in its life it happened to be.

Lords and Princes, Grandfather Shadow had missed this one. Unfortunately, he also knew that the wolf and all his kind had turned away from him after the Battle of Kyrtigaen Pass. Grandfather Shadow had to tread carefully, or things might be very bad for Julianna.

"You knew I'd be here?" Grandfather Shadow asked.

The wolf nodded.

"You know what I want."

The wolf nodded.

"And knowing you, it's some where or when I cannot reach."

Again, a nod.

"Will you give it to me?"

The wolf just looked at him. Grandfather Shadow knew better than to try and wait out this particular wolf.

"Razka, please," Grandfather Shadow said. "I could not have done anything at Kyrtigaen pass. I wanted to. Think of how it was for me, trapped in the mind of an idiot that never should have been named Lord Morigahn, never mind how he ever managed to survive the trial."

When the wolf did not react, Grandfather Shadow decided that a bit of waiting wouldn't hurt. As it was, he'd waited a thousand years; he could wait a little while longer.

For a long time the wolf and the god regarded each other. Each moment took them closer to the moment the knife would reach the perfect heat. Also, there was no guarantee that someone or something with malicious intent wouldn't come along and find Julianna helpless. Sloppy. He'd been so sloppy and careless. He could have hidden her in Illusion, or made it so anyone arriving there could have no Knowledge of her presence.

"Unlike some others," Grandfather Shadow said, "I do not have all the time in existence. I have to return to the new Lord Morigahn soon, or she may be discovered."

The wolf's ear twitched, and its head cocked to the side.

"Oh, yes," Grandfather Shadow said. "I've decided to name a woman. Perhaps you know her, Duchess Julianna Taraen of House Kolmonen."

The wolf growled at him, deep and menacing.

"Spare me, Razka," Grandfather Shadow said. "You may be bitter. You may be angry, and yes, I told you this in order to manipulate you into doing what I want. I don't have time to stroke your pride or nurse your old wounds. Julianna waits in a half-sleep for me to return. I will mark her, and set her upon the Lord Morigahn's path. It's your choice if she walks that path fully armed."

The wolf vanished in a ripple of localized lightning. A small clap of thunder echoed a moment later. That could be either good or bad. Either way, Grandfather Shadow didn't want to wait any longer. If Razka had decided to help, Julianna would get what she needed when Razka decided it was time.

When he returned to the fire, Grandfather Shadow found the knife blade glowing red. Picking up the knife, he examined the blade. It was too sharp, so he picked up a rock and ran it across the knife's edge seven times, dulling the blade. Grandfather Shadow returned to Julianna and released her from the half-sleep. She looked from his eyes to the glowing blade. She tried to back away, but Grandfather Shadow grabbed her.

"This is going to hurt." He would never lie to her again.

Julianna screamed as the knife cut down her face. She struggled, but the god was too strong. As the blade bit deeper and deeper into her flesh, the god spoke words in that strange tongue, and Julianna felt the knife pass through her physical form and into her spirit. A bond formed between her and Grandfather Shadow, and the heated blade became a bridge between them. He leaned in close to her and whispered in her ear. His voice carried the words, but she received the god's information from where the knife penetrated her soul.

All the knowledge and secrets of the Lord Morigahn swam in Julianna's head, though not all of it came from Grandfather Shadow. There were some fragments of memories that came from her own childhood that she had only remembered in her deepest dreams. She had learned much of *Galad'laman* as a child, and then she had forgotten. She tried to make some sense of it all, but there was too much. Each time she pulled something to the front of her mind, all the rest would crowd around it, as if seeking Julianna's attention.

"The pain will fade faster than you think," Grandfather Shadow said. "In time, you will grow accustomed to both the knowledge and the scar. Now, gather the Morigahnti, find the heir to the seven mountains, and reclaim Koma's once great empire."

Grandfather Shadow finished marking Julianna, took Khellan's *Galad'fana*, and wrapped the gray cloth around her head. He would have preferred her to have the same holy cloth that he had given to Kaeldyr so many centuries before, but that would have to wait until Razka decided it was time for her to have it.

He had given the Lord Morigahn everything she needed to lead the Morigahnti. Everything, except a guardian.

Looking out through every shadow in the world, Grandfather Shadow found the perfect man to protect Julianna.

Only one problem remained. The man was still alive.

Grandfather Shadow sent lightning crashing down from the sky, and just as the mortal's life ended, the god channeled a small portion of his divinity into the man.

"I name you the Sentinel," Grandfather Shadow said.

Then he moved the man hundreds of miles to the northeast and laid him against a tree in the apple orchard. Best to give the young man a bit of time to acclimate to the sudden change.

Having taken care of everything he could think of for the moment, Grandfather Shadow paused for reflection. The King of Order's prison had been meant to teach the Greater Gods humility. Grandfather Shadow had acted just as he had during the Second War of the Gods. If he wasn't careful, he might wind up back in his prison. Should that happen, Julianna would never survive, much less lead the Komati people back to him.

The world had changed. Grandfather Shadow needed to change with it. Subtlety, something none of the greater gods had ever been adept at, was required. For now, Grandfather Shadow would wait and assist Julianna only when she asked him. Perhaps he might send her a boon when she really needed one. If she was truly all Grandfather Shadow hoped, she wouldn't need his help very often, especially with the Sentinel by her side.

SIX

A cauldron bubbled in a secret chamber in the Governor's Palace of Koma city. Octavio Salvatore, the First Adept of Old Uncle Night, ground his teeth as the mists from the cauldron dissipated. For the most part, Octavio considered himself a man of even temper, but now he fought the urge to reach out and break something. True, there were moments when he doled out punishments terrible in severity, but when that happened, it was out of necessity, not fury.

This disaster could not have come at a worse time. The Brotherhood of the Night was about to seize control of the Kingdom of the Sun, and part of that aim required that the Morigahnti remain quietly in the background. An unauthorized attack on any Morigahnti and the murder of the Lord Morigahn broke all agreements Octavio had made with his few contacts within the Morigahnti.

The doors to the Chapel of Night opened. Dante, Octavio's younger brother by six years, entered, wearing a self-satisfied smirk while his dark eyes glimmered with a secret. He wore these expressions more and more frequently as the years passed. Dante possessed the gift of prophecy and foresight. While any who saw visions and spoke prophesies were sought after by all the Great Houses, it usually took these individuals years to understand their gifts well enough to assess the predictions with any accuracy. This was not so with Dante. Within minutes of speaking a prophecy, he understood with alarming regularity what his gift had told him of the future. In addition, his youth gave him an arrogance that he wore like a garment. Dante only removed that garment in front of the Sun King, the Speaker of the Sun, and occasionally Octavio. This was not one of those times.

"Do you know anything about this?" Octavio gestured at the cauldron.

Dante swaggered over and glanced at the bloody scene revealed in the mist.

"I ordered it," Dante replied as if he were replying to a question about the seating placements at a banquet or the choices of refreshments at a ball.

"What?" Octavio's hands clenched into fists. "Why?" He opened his hands; it was a struggle not to wrap them around Dante's neck. "We had an agreement with them."

Dante traced his finger along the edge of the cauldron. "An agreement we were planning to break as soon as it was convenient for us."

"Yes. But once we secured the throne."

"But it was necessary for us to kill the Lord Morigahn now," Dante replied. "The Morigahnti had no intentions of holding to the agreement either, and I'm surprised that you believed they would. Now they will be in a state of chaos until well after we have secured the Brotherhood's control of the Kingdom."

To emphasize his point, Dante thrust his finger into the water. Ripples disrupted the water and caused the vision within to warp and fade.

Octavio said. "Did your prophecy tell you anything of a new Lord Morigahn being named today?"

Seeing Dante's face break from his usual all-knowing mask was almost worth this development – yes, think of this as a development rather than a disaster. A moment later, Dante's lips shifted from a gaping circle of surprise back to a wide grin.

"Nearly had me there, Octavio," Dante said. "But it will take the Morigahnti months to gather in order to choose a new leader."

"Not anymore. The new Lord Morigahn freed Grandfather Shadow. He named her himself."

Dante's face fell again. "Gods and goddesses." He took a deep breath. "Wait. Did you say *her*?"

"Yes." Octavio waved his hand over the cauldron. The waters smoothed, and Octavio shifted the view to focus in on the woman cupping her hands over her face. "That is the new Lord Morigahn, Duchess Julianna Taraen."

"Taraen. Didn't we—?"

"Yes," Octavio said. "Do you see why this creates an entirely new situation we must deal with on many different levels? It may be as you say, that it will take time for them to organize under her, but I would rather have some idea of what the future will bring. Until you can bring me some good news, I want you to clean the chapel while I—"

"Me? Why not one of the disciples? That's what they're for."

"It's always good to remember where you came from, little brother."

"Then why don't you clean it?" Dante snapped.

"Because I have a Kingdom protectorate to govern," Octavio said. "And I am not the one who possibly ruined years of careful planning."

"I haven't," Dante said, "My speaking clearly—"

Octavio raised his hand. "You did not foresee this new Lord Morigahn, much less Grandfather Shadow coming to personally name her."

Leaving Dante in the Chapel of Night, Octavio pondered how to solve the problems this new Lord Morigahn posed. He wasn't even going to consider the ramifications of Grandfather Shadow himself being freed when none of the other gods had been. It seemed Dante didn't want to either, or it would have come up. It was much easier to focus on mortal dilemmas, leaving the celestial and infernal realms to deal with each other.

The biggest problem with Julianna Taraen was that Octavio could not act directly, or his ties to Old Uncle Night might be discovered. Fortunately, he had many strings to pull and pawns to play, most of which he could deploy through layers and layers of contacts and allies so that it would be nearly impossible to follow the path back to him. And if somebody did begin to deduce the true mastermind behind the events, well, it wouldn't be the first corpse Octavio had left in his wake. Assassination, lies, treachery, and extortion were the weapons of choice in the battle for Zenith of the Throne. All the Houses used these tools. There were only two ways for one House to take the Zenith away from another. One involved a considerable number of political marriages, and the other requireed many deaths. Of course, the Brotherhood of the Night preferred the second.

Just outside the chapel, Octavio saw Kavala, Dante's bodyguard. Kavala leaned against a wall, head down with the hood of his dark cloak pulled down low over his face. He held a pipe in his mouth and puffed on the stem. The hood hid the man's mangled face. Scars of some torture endured long ago marred Kavala so much that seeing his face made Octavio's stomach churn. However, Kavala had been a gift from Old Uncle Night's wife, sent to insure Dante's safety, so Octavio endured Kavala's deformity.

"Good evening, Your Darkness," Kavala said.

At least Dante's dog had manners, which was more than Octavio could say for his younger brother. If nothing else, Kavala knew his place and remained ever respectful of Octavio's status both as a Duke of the Realm and as First Adept of Old Uncle Night.

"I'm sorry to say you may remain there for some time yet," Octavio said.

"I have no pressing engagements, Your Grace," Kavala replied with a bow.

Octavio nodded. He needed to think, and for that, he needed his wife. She would get him to relax, and then he would talk to her. She would sit there and listen, as she always did, and might even interject an idea or two, until some form of plan came to Octavio.

SEVEN

A few moments after Yrgaeshkil felt the scrying from Octavio's cauldron vanish, a small flash of lighting illuminated the air next to Julianna; a clap of thunder roared less than a heartbeat later. A man dressed all in furs and leathers, hair wild and snarled, leaned over Julianna. He watched her trembling and crying for a time, much longer than Yrgaeshkil had ever seen any of his kind remain still.

Yrgaeshkil knew him. She'd known him for a long time. Like with so many Minor Eldar who could not be commanded by their names, she hadn't bothered to remember his.

The man reached down, placed his hand on Julianna's head, and gently stroked her hair.

"I'm sorry," he said.

Then the man stood and faced Yrgaeshkil. "You forgot smell. Don't worry. No one is watching."

Yrgaeshkil dropped the Lie completely.

"I forgot how crafty you people are," the goddess said.

"We are what we are," the man replied. "Just as you, we act and react according to our nature."

"I have no quarrel with you," Yrgaeshkil said.

He snorted a sound halfway between a laugh and a growl. "And I believe you, why? The Mother of Daemyns and Goddess of Lies."

"I would shake off both of those mantles if I could."

"Would you?"

"Indeed."

"Again, I believe you, why?"

Yrgaeshkil shrugged. "What do you want?"

"To warn you," the man said. "You have toyed with her enough. Leave off. If you don't, I will become displeased."

Suddenly, her wolf-skin mantle felt a bit warm and uncomfortable.

"Are you threatening me?" Yrgaeshkil couldn't believe his audacity.

"I am."

She opened her mouth to say something, but words failed her. This lesser being, barely even a Minor Eldar, was threatening her who had given birth to the multitudes of Daemynic species.

"Don't know quite how to take that?" This time he did laugh, an amused chuckle from deep in his belly. "Been a long time, has it? Well, I know that I might not be able to do much to you, myself, but I and my kind can be anywhere we need to in order to know your plans and upset them. You may eventually strike us all down, and you may wear our skins as mantles, or make boots out of them, or whatever suits your whim at the moment. But not before we ensure that every scheme you have for the next thousand years turns against you."

How she wanted to end him, to destroy him utterly and completely, but she couldn't ensure that she'd be fast enough. If he got away, a war between the Stormseekers and Daemyns would erupt across the realms. While the Stormseekers could not hope to win that war, it would be costly indeed, and she could not afford the distraction with Grandfather Shadow roaming free.

"Very well," Yrgaeshkil said. "Do you mind if I watch?"

"Do what you will, so long as you leave her be."

Lightning flashed. Thunder roared. He was gone and appeared again, this time carrying a massive book. It could only be the *Galad'parma.* The man pushed the book underneath Julianna. She wrapped her arms around it as if she were drowning and it could save her. It might very well save her, Yrgaeshkil thought.

He looked at Yrgaeshkil. The lighting and thunder came again, and he was gone and did not return.

Yrgaeshkil leaned against the oak and covered herself with a Lie, this time masking scent as well.

EIGHT

Luciano Salvatore, Adept of All Father Sun and Inquisitor of House Floraen, woke with a start as his prized possession buzzed and chimed him awake. He sat up, rubbing the sleep from his eyes. He and his younger cousin Santo, who was also an Inquisitor, had decided to camp in a copse of trees by a stream rather than avail themselves of the hospitality of the local Komati nobility. Luciano had reports that several of the local families illegally worshiped Grandfather Shadow. Staying at the wrong estate could find them both the surprised recipients of slit throats.

"What is it?" Santo ask.

"Something's happening," Luciano rifled through his pack, which he'd been using as a pillow. After a few moments he found it.

He called the thing The Detector, which most people, at least the few who ever saw it, mistook for a pocket watch. Any similarities The Detector might have to a pocket watch were purely cosmetic. It had hands, but five rather than two. Instead of numbers, the apparatus had five symbols, one for each of the greater gods. In the presence of divine power, the device would chime. The closer the divine power that was being channeled, the louder the chimes rang. If divine power had been channeled in an area but was being channeled no longer, The Detector would vibrate. When Luciano opened the gold and silver device in the presence of divine power, one of the hands would point to that god's symbol – the larger the hand, the stronger the source of divine power. To date, the largest hand had not moved from the blank spot that twelve o'clock normally occupied on normal clocks.

Today was different. The two largest hands, including the one that had never moved, pointed to Grandfather Shadow's symbol. The middle hand pointed to Old Uncle Night.

"Well?" asked his cousin.

"Look for yourself." Luciano handed him The Detector.

"Two hands for one god? Has that ever happened before?"

"No."

Santo handed The Detector back.

"What can it mean?"

"I couldn't even begin to speculate." Luciano continued staring at those two hands pointing at Grandfather Shadow's symbol – especially the one hand that had never moved before. He sighed.

"What's wrong?" Santo asked.

Luciano looked at his cousin, fresh to the Inquisitors, full of zeal, and eager to prove himself worthy of the title. How long ago had it been since Luciano had felt like that? It seemed a lifetime, when in truth, he'd only been an Inquisitor for nine years. Nine years of fighting Morigahnti, and Daemyn worshipers, and those firearm-toting madmen of northern Heidenmarch. He could just imagine Santo's heart beating with excitement at the prospect of discovering the source of this oddity that The Detector had discovered. Every fresh Inquisitor Luciano had ever known, himself included, always wanted to be the one who discovered some terrible new threat to the Kingdom of the Sun. They were all idiots, Luciano included. The ones who grew out of that idiocy were the ones that survived.

"Nothing." Luciano said. "I suppose we'll have to investigate to find out."

Santo's entire face grinned like some child going off to fair for the first time. "Of course we will!"

They broke camp and dressed as quickly as they could.

"Santo," Luciano said, as he helped strap his cousin's breastplate into place. "I need you to listen."

"Of course," Santo said. "I always listen to your wisdom and value your experience."

"No. You are lying." Santo opened his mouth to protest, but Luciano held his hand up to quiet him. Santo had seen the gesture enough times to recognize its meaning. "You're not intentionally lying, but you are lying all the same. I did it as well when I was fresh to the Inquisitors. The most important Truth to know is the Truth within ourselves. When we know that, All Father Sun will bless us as he blesses no other, and the lies of the world cannot take hold of our minds, hearts, or spirits."

"I'm not afraid." Santo said. "I will not fall victim to Old Uncle Night's lies."

"Fear is a part of life," Luciano said, "just as death comes for all men. Each god and goddess has a place in the world, and reality would crumble without their control over the dominion. By not acknowledging our fear, we fall victim to the lies we tell ourselves, and those are the most dangerous lies of all, the hardest lies to see beyond.

"We are also only two. We do not share the Father's full blessing without a third, and so, we must be doubly cautious, especially should we meet an enemy whose numbers coincide with their deity's numbers."

"Yes, Luciano," Santo replied. "I understand."

But the young man didn't. He looked the part of the stoic Inquisitor, sitting stiff and straight in his saddle, but that was only because it was what he was taught, what was expected. Were they riding through a town, Luciano would have assumed the same, authoritative pose. However, out here, on a road far between towns, where the Komati nobility kept their summer estates, most of which would be empty this close to autumn anyway, Luciano didn't bother with the pretense of appearances.

As they rode to investigate this mystery, Luciano quietly prayed for All Father Sun to open Santo's eyes to the Truth within himself.

NINE

Faelin woke with a start. His heart pounded hard in his chest, and his breath came in quick gasps. For a moment he had felt as if he was on fire, but now the pain was gone. It must have been a dream. He forced himself to breathe at a steady pace.

He noticed two things right away. First was that the air was a bit colder than it should have been at dawn. Second, the scent of apples filled the air. More changes to his world came after that. He was leaning against a tree. When he'd gone to sleep, he'd lain out under a tree in a field of tall grass – now he was at the very edge of an orchard.

Faelin suppressed the urge to jump to his feet and draw his rapier. If someone had wanted to kill him, they certainly would have done so. No, it wasn't death that had come for him but some other power.

Rather than jump around in a panic, Faelin got up slowly, stretched, and pulled the small, palm-sized journal out of the secret pocket in his left boot. He flipped through it until he came to the words he wanted. He'd managed to memorize very little of the *fyrmest spaeg geoda*, but he'd made extensive notes of statements he could make and what their uses were. He studied the one he wanted for a few moments, making sure of the pronunciations.

"*Kahhdria ekbilak jyvmirjy*," Faelin said.

A rush of winds surrounded him, warm and cold buffeted against his skin and whipped at his clothes. A moment later, a beautiful young woman stood a few paces away. She was naked, but a continuous breeze containing dust, leaves, and twigs spun around her, covering the more distracting parts of her body. This morning her hair was a deep platinum-blond with just a hint of the whitish-blue that hung on the horizons at the height of spring.

He hadn't expected her to appear so soon. This sudden arrival meant she must have been close by. However, with Khaddria, that could mean within a few hundred leagues.

"I really hate it when you do that," the goddess of wind said.

"I'm not too fond of being made a pawn in your games again," Faelin replied.

"I'm not…" Kahddria trailed off.

She looked him up and down, floated in a circle around him. Faelin felt like a prize piece of livestock being examined at a country fair.

"What?" Faelin asked.

"You've changed," Kahddria said. "And you aren't even aware of how much you've changed."

"I'm not in the mood for games, goddess," Faelin said, flipping the pages in his journal.

"I'm not playing any games. Well, at least not with you. I'm playing against much bigger players with much higher stakes."

"Tell me," Faelin said.

Kahddria stopped circling when she came back in front of Faelin. She crossed her arms and actually settled her feet on the earth. "You may have that little book and my promise to do you no harm," Kahddria said, "but that's not going to motivate me to betray the secrets of others who frighten me much more than any temporary annoyance you might be. Good morning Faelin vara'Traejyn. It was nice to see you again, even if you interrupted a very important conversation. May your summers and winters be short, springs be mild, and autumn reaping plentiful."

The wind around them started picking up, meaning she was about to depart. Faelin considered forcing her to stay and answer his questions, but after a moment he rejected the thought. The goddess might not be able to hurt him, but that didn't mean she couldn't arrange for life to be very difficult.

"Oh. You'll want to go that way." She gestured toward the east. "Once you get to the stream and mill, I'm sure you'll recognize your surroundings."

With that, she vanished into the wind.

"Damn," Faelin muttered. What had he gotten himself involved in this time?

Well, he saw no reason to put off figuring out what was going on. Faelin packed his camp, which didn't take long, as whoever had moved him here, hadn't bothered to bring anything other than his blanket and pack. His food bag, tied in a tree, and cooking utensils had remained in Heidenmarch. He chuckled to himself as he imagined some passerby walking along the road and finding the remains of the camp. With his journal back in his boot and his pack and bedroll slung across his shoulders, Faelin started walking.

As soon as he came to the mill and saw the towering oak tree at the top of the hill, Faelin recognized Kaeldyr's Rest. Ravens circled the oak.

Faelin drew in a deep breath and let it out very slowly. He'd suspected he'd be in Koma, but had hoped that maybe, just maybe, he'd been drawn to some other place. And of all the places in Koma it could be, it had to be Kaeldyr's Rest. Nothing good could come from climbing that hill. He ran his hands through his hair and looked about, noticing a few crossbow bolts scattered about the ground outside of the mill. Looking closer, he saw the bloodstains in the earth. He hurried to one of the windows, glanced in, and saw pools of blood on the stone floor.

The only people he could imagine fighting a battle here were the Morigahnti. But who would they be fighting against? Faelin supposed it didn't matter. They were either still here, or they weren't. If they were, he'd figure out a way to deal with it. No matter what the gods threw at him, he always managed to scrape through.

Despite the amount of blood spilled, the mill was clear of bodies. He looked up the hill toward the ancient oak tree and the ravens circling in the air.

As he went up the hill, Faelin drew his rapier. He'd considered leaving his pack and bedroll hidden by the mill, but reconsidered. They helped to add credibility to his strange and sudden appearance, and they might be stolen. Replacing his cooking gear would be bad enough.

At the top of the hill, Faelin discovered the remains of a small battle. Dozens of bodies littered the earth around a great oak tree, many of them skinned alive. Panic threatened to overwhelm him, but Faelin forced himself to remain calm. This was not the first time in his life strange things had occurred with seemingly no explanation. He gave a quick prayer, partially for the fallen and partially for luck not to get drawn into a game between deities again. Something told Faelin that only the first part of his prayer would be answered.

Something moved next to him. Faelin jumped away and brought his rapier to bear. A woman in the tattered remains of a lady's riding dress writhed on the ground. The only garment she wore that wasn't in tatters was a dark gray scarf wrapped around her head. It looked almost like a *Galad'fana*, one of the wrappings the Morigahnti wore in their worship of Grandfather Shadow.

Faelin scanned the other bodies in case someone else was feigning death, waiting in ambush for an unsuspecting, kindhearted soul. The remnants of black leather armor lay in tatters around the skinned bodies, except for one, who wore the black robes of an Adept of Old Uncle Night.

Some of the other bodies wore coats cut in the Komati fashion, decorated with House and family colors. But more than that, each one had a long gray cloth wrapped around his neck. Those veils were *Galad'fana*, making the men Morigahnti.

Faelin swatted at the flies buzzing around him and looked beyond the gruesome scene now that he was on top of the hill. He saw horses, many of them saddled, grazing in the fields around hill. Some of them were Saifreni, though most had the look of Standard Blood working horses, probably for the rank and file of the Brotherhood of the Night.

Finding no obvious threats, Faelin sheathed his rapier and glanced at the single survivor of the battle. As he got closer, he saw that the girl actually was wearing a *Galad'fana*. Her pained moans pulled at his heart. Faelin wanted to reach out to her, but he had to know if any miracles or other surprises were lingering about.

"*Aeteowian ic seo wat sodlis ikona*," Faelin said. That was one phrase he knew by heart.

The ancient first tongue of creation was lost to all but a few scholarly orders. Unlike the divine languages of the greater gods, the *fyrmest spaeg geo-*

da did not have the power to perform miracles. It only revealed the presence of celestial powers or creatures.

The moment Faelin spoke, words appeared written in the air. Some were in the spidery script of Grandfather Shadow's language. Others were the dizzying, sweeping loops of Old Uncle Night's. The *Galad'fana* and the Adept's robe glowed from the small bits of divine power blessed into them. All these images began fading almost immediately, indicating that the words in the air representing recently spoken miracles had all taken effect. There were no surprises waiting.

As these letters faded, Faelin studied them, trying to tell where each had originated. Each miracle had a thin bond with the divine focus that had been used to channel it into existence, and each one connected with one of the *Galad'fana* worn by the Morigahnti. Some of the miracles in Old Uncle Night's language had been spoken by people no longer present.

"Wait a moment," Faelin said to himself.

He should have seen them before, but there were so many other words hanging in the air, that Faelin had missed the few that had no ties to any foci. Those words could have only been spoken from the lips of pure faith, without the use of a divine focus. Nobody in any land had spoken a miracle of pure faith in centuries. The girl had spoken one of those miracles, but whoever had spoken the others was gone. Faelin looked closer. He saw that someone else had spoken through the girl.

Reaching into his boot, he brought out his journal. After a few moments of rifling through the pages, he found what he was looking for. He read the passage several times in his head, mouthing to practice forming the words.

When he felt he had it well enough not to butcher it, Faelin said, "*Audsyna egni hinn hulaetur.*"

Three ghostly forms appeared. One hovered above a pile of dust, the second lay in the same spot as the girl, the third stood in the same place as one of the Komati men. The first had a human's body, leathery wings, and a bat-like head with ram's horns sprouting from behind its ears. The other two ghostly images looked human. However, the one sharing space with the girl had some small aspect of divinity bound to it; that must have been what had spoken the miracle through the girl. The third spectral form caused Faelin to step back. The truth of its origin was well hidden, but ultimately could not hide from the primal power of *fyrmest spaeg geoda.* It was Grandfather Shadow, walking free on the physical realm. Somehow, a soul from the Realm of Shadows had given the girl enough faith to free Grandfather Shadow from his prison.

Faelin chewed on his lip. Grandfather Shadow was free. Were any of the other greater gods? No, he could not think about that. There were too many frightening possibilities down that path, and Faelin had often been accused of having too much imagination for his own good. He returned to the image of Grandfather Shadow. Was that who had put Faelin here? If so, why? The girl was the only thing he could think of.

"Are you hurt?" Faelin asked, kneeling next to her.

She made a sound part way between a scream and a growl and pulled away. As she scurried backwards, the girl slashed at the air between them with a dagger. The movement caused her to drop a large book and the veil to come away from her face.

Faelin read the title and gaped. *Galad'parma.* The Tome of Shadows, Grandfather Shadow's holy book. This volume was larger than any Faelin had ever seen. His heart pounded as pieces began to fall together. No, the gods had not answered his second prayer.

Looking from the book to the girl, Faelin saw a deep gash running down the right side of her face, glowing with divine power. That wound confirmed his fears. Grandfather Shadow had marked this girl as the new Lord Morigahn.

Taking in the rest of the poor girl's face, Faelin recognized her. She'd been sixteen and was growing into a lovely young woman when he saw her last. He hadn't thought about her in years. She would be twenty-one now. Actually, twenty-one as of yesterday. The years had been good to her. Aside from that scar, she possessed more beauty than any three women had rights to.

"Julianna?" he asked. "Is that you?"

Her steel-gray eyes darted back and forth, trying to look everywhere at once, but she kept the dagger leveled between them.

"Julianna," he repeated. "It's Faelin. Don't you remember me?"

Her gaze rested on his face. She nodded slightly. He stepped forward, but she raised the knife. Thin wisps of smoke rose from the blade, as if it had been heated in the fire.

"I want to help you, Julianna. Can you talk to me?"

Her mouth opened, and her head moved forward slightly. Her lips looked as if they were trying to form words, and her eyes rolled up a bit, as if she were trying to gaze into her own mind. She took a deep breath and closed her eyes. When she opened them again, her head and shoulders slumped forward and her eyes fixed on her feet.

"*Ji*," she finally whispered, sounding utterly defeated.

The word was *yes* in *Galad'laman*, the language of Grandfather Shadow. Faelin's father had taught him the forbidden tongue. How could Julianna have learned it?

"I'm going to look around," Faelin said. "Then we're leaving."

Faelin went over to the man closest to Julianna. Turning the body over, Faelin recognized his old friend, Khellan Dubhan. Khellan also bore a scar like the one on Julianna's face, except that Khellan's scar had healed some time ago. In the right pocket of his waistcoat, Khellan had a pocket watch. Such a device was a blatant symbol of hatred for the Kingdom. Though pocket watches were legal, the Kingdom usually kept a close eye on the possessor for fear of what other suspicious or outlawed technology they might own.

Faelin had walked away from any contact with the Morigahnti long ago, vowing to never deal with them again, choosing to follow Grandfather Shadow in his own way instead. He looked at Julianna, alone and half mad. He couldn't leave her to face the journey before her. Deep in his heart, Faelin was Grandfather Shadow's servant. Morigahnti be damned, he would walk this road next to her. Julianna would need someone to protect her, teach her about the Morigahnti, and explain the subtleties of Grandfather Shadow's laws. Faelin didn't know if he was the one to teach her; it had been so long since he'd spoken to a Morigahnti, much less been a part of their rituals, but he couldn't imagine the infighting and politicking having died out in the last few years. He glanced at Khellan's body. No, it had not died out. While Faelin had liked Khellan, and the young lord might have the scar of a Lord Morigahn, he was no *Morigahnti'uljas*, Lord of the Morigahnti. Somehow, someone must have managed to determine a way to cheat the trials.

Well, that was a question and a challenge for another day. For now, he had to get them both as far from this place as possible. With the amount of divine energy that had been flung around, not to mention one of the greater gods having been freed from his prison, Faelin didn't want to guess who or what might arrive to investigate.

He rummaged through the remains of the picnic. He found a basket of pears and apples, the perfect thing for tempting horses. He wouldn't be able to get them too close to the gory scene at the top of the hill, but a little closer and gathered together was better than nothing. With the basket under his left arm, Faelin went hunting horses.

At first, he headed toward a group gathered close to each other in the fields below the hill, but then movement near the apple orchard caught his eye. There, in the shade of the trees, was a familiar black and white animal. The last time Faelin had seen that particular horse, it had barely been old enough to ride, and now it had grown into quite the monster, but those markings hadn't changed enough to make it unrecognizable. He couldn't help but smile. That horse might very well make it possible to get Julianna calm enough to ride from this place. And, if Faelin remembered correctly, he had the perfect bait to trap that prey.

The apples in the basket worked even better than he'd hoped, and Vendyr seemed to remember him. Faelin spent a good ten to fifteen minutes feeding Vendyr and stroking the animal's neck and face, especially around the ears, eyes, and nostrils, gently caressing those areas to build intimacy between him and the horse as Vendyr kept his muzzle in the basket, happily munching on the apples and pears. Faelin shook his head. Even before he'd fled, this horse had been the most food-motivated animal Faelin had ever known. It was good to see that some things, the simple things, did not change.

Once he'd created the beginnings of a relationship with Vendyr, he used the horse to collect others. Horses were natural followers, inclined to group together. Vendyr was a dominant animal. Even at two and three, Faelin recalled the horse challenging older horses. He used Vendyr to gather up four of the other horses, selecting those that were already saddled.

Things became more difficult when Faelin took them closer to the carnage at the top of the hill. The trouble with herd animals was that when one started spooking and the rest of them caught onto it, the feeling spread like a plague, only faster. It took Faelin the better part of an hour to get them even halfway up the hill. He practiced steady breathing techniques to calm himself, but even still, he just wanted to punch the horses. To keep them from wandering off, he'd taken the basket that he'd used to bribe Vendyr, filled it with apples from the orchard, and scattered the fruit on the ground at the point where the horses refused to go any higher.

Finally, his hands raw and muscles sore from fighting with the horses, Faelin had the animals chomping away about halfway up the hill. Faelin prepared Vendyr for riding, taking tack and saddle from a collection gathered at a point partway down the hill. Likely, the servants had been sent here while the lords and ladies enjoyed themselves by the oak. That's how it had been when Faelin had been invited to join them so many years ago. Hoping the scattered apples would help keep the horses from wandering too far, Faelin went back up the hill.

First, Faelin scavenged the camp. He put the Tome of Shadows in his backpack, collected some usable clothes from the Komati lords, and gathered up what food he thought would travel well: bread and cheeses mostly, and some dried fruit. He considered taking the weapons and perhaps selling them along the way, but he wanted as little to do with the Brotherhood of the Night as possible. And someone selling that many weapons would be remembered. He settled on three rapiers, even though he already had one. That gave them two blades apiece. He hoped Julianna had kept up practice with her swordplay. As the Lord Morigahn, she needed to learn to handle a blade better than he remembered she could. The only other thing of value he found was a small purse filled with gold and silver coins. He collected all the *Galad'fana* and stuffed them in his backpack with the *Galad'parma.* Those were not items to be left for any passersby to stumble upon. With that in mind, he stoked the fire back to life, took the mantle from the Adept of Old Uncle Night, and tossed it on the fire. Faint snarls and cries of pain whispered out of the smoke and flames as the cloth burned.

Now the hard part began.

"Julianna," Faelin said softly.

She jerked at the sound of her name, shifting to keep the dagger between them.

"I'm not going to hurt you. I got your horse ready so we can leave this place. Look. There's Vendyr."

When Faelin said Vendyr's name, Julianna stood and looked down the hill. Her eyes brightened a bit.

"Listen carefully," Faelin said to Julianna. "I'm going to help you onto Vendyr. We need to be away from this place as soon as possible."

Julianna nodded. She dropped the dagger and let him help her to her feet. Faelin picked up the dagger and handed it back to her.

"You might need this later," he said.

She took the blade and held it close.

Faelin managed to help her into a coat that covered most of her tattered clothes, and then led her down the hill. Getting her onto Vendyr was easier than he's expected. She almost flew into the saddle.

Faelin mounted and gave one last look at the bodies at the top of the hill. It wrenched at his heart that he could not perform the Ritual of Sending, but he had never learned it. Even the Nightbrothers deserved better than to have their spirits wallowing here. Hopefully someone would come along who would be able to perform the ritual so the souls here had a better chance of ascending to one of the gods' celestial realms rather than being cast down into the Dark Realm of the Godless Dead.

Turning his horse, he led Julianna and the spare mounts away from the sun. His plan was to flee Koma before the Kingdom or the Morigahnti found them. They would stay away for as long as it took for Julianna to learn what it meant to be the Lord Morigahn. Faelin set a brisk pace; they needed to cover ground as fast as possible. If the Brotherhood of the Night found Julianna, death would likely be the least of their worries.

TEN

Luciano and Santo Salvatore reached Kaeldyr's Rest just before noon. They first noticed the air and trees filled with crows or ravens, Luciano could never remember which. He wondered if any happened to be those blasted birds that the Morigahnti associated with. True, the followers of all the gods made pacts with various spirit animals, but the Inquisitors knew the truth, that these creatures were not actually divine in nature, and thus steered as far from them as possible.

As they rode up the hill, their horses trained not to balk at anything, the sickly-sweet hint of rotting flesh hung in the air. Bodies of Komati and Nightbrother, as well as a few horses, littered the ground surrounding a giant oak tree. Both Inquisitors dismounted and withdrew their ruby pendants from underneath their mantles. These chains of office, gold with bright rubies the size of lemons at the center, declared them not only House Floraen Inquisitors but also that they were acting in the official capacity of their office.

After just a few moments, Luciano pieced together the conflict between the Brotherhood of the Night and the Morigahnti. He marveled at how many of the Brotherhood the Morigahnti had managed to kill. He also wondered which side had ultimately won.

"Luciano," Santo said, as he circled the gruesome scene. "I've found a few trails leading off."

Santo was a natural tracker. He understood the comings and goings of men and beasts over terrain in much the way a virtuoso musician could play a song perfectly after hearing it once. Luciano possessed a similar gift, in that he could determine much about the way someone died by examining the corpse and its surroundings, but for some reason he couldn't translate that ability into tracking the way Santo could.

Luciano went over to his cousin.

"A large group went that way," Santo pointed southeast. "And there is a second."

Even Luciano could see the trampled grass and multitude of horse prints now that Santo showed him. Luciano took The Detector and walked about twenty-seven paces in the wake of that trail. The symbol of Old Uncle Night glowed, and the middle hand pointed toward that symbol.

"Where's the other," Luciano asked, as he returned.

Santo took him to the other side of the hill and pointed at something on the ground Luciano couldn't see.

"Just point me in the direction of the path and tell me if it turns," Luciano said.

"There." Santo adjusted Luciano's shoulders so he faced almost due west. "It doesn't turn."

Luciano walked twenty-seven paces along that path. When he stoped, the symbol of Grandfather Shadow – with the first two hands pointing toward it – glowed when he held it out.

"Which do we follow?" Santo asked.

Luciano tilted his head from side to side, as if he were a scale coming into balance. "Both might be pertinent to the security of the realm."

"But two hands?" they said it at the same time.

They gave each other the same sidelong glance, complete with a lopsided smile. Both had become Inquisitors because they wanted to solve mysteries that threatened the Kingdom. There was still so little known about the protectorates and the world beyond the Kingdom's borders. So much of it was hostile, and keen minds had been needed to puzzle these mysteries out.

"We could split up," Santo said. "Toss a coin and see where chance takes us."

Luciano glanced down at The Detector. A third hand shifted toward the symbol of Grandfather Shadow, and it glowed even brighter. He sucked in a quick breath.

"What is it?" Santo asked.

Luciano handed The Detector over.

"Well, that decides it." Santo spoke in a hushed tone as if he were witnessing a miracle spoken by pure faith and not one through a foci. "We have to discover what this means."

"Agreed." Luciano said.

ELEVEN

Yrgaeshkil smiled as the two Inquisitors rode away.

True, she had promised Razka that she would not harm Julianna. Yrgaeshkil believed him and his threats. However, the world was a dangerous place for anyone bearing the title of the Lord Morigahn: the Inquisitors of House Floraen being among the most ruthless and tenacious threats. It was the simplest thing to manipulate the enchanted device to ensure those two Inquisitors followed Julianna. With any luck, the Inquisitors would take Julianna by surprise and kill her. What did it matter if that protector was a Saent when the two Inquisitors were armed with Faerii steel?

HUNTER AND HUNTED

Octavio,

An Inquisitor just left my cell. His smug arrogance filled the room, and he spoke and carried himself as though expecting me to beg for my life. It amazes me how Adepts of the other Houses believe that execution could punish a servant of the God of Death. Do not weep for me, dear cousin, I yearn for Old Uncle Night's embrace.

Do not think that I hold any malice toward you. You made the right choice. It was not the Brotherhood's time, and I applaud your patience. I believe the Brotherhood's time will come, and when it does, I am confident that you will be the Night King. However, be warned: some Brothers will try to lead you down an evil path. Let your ears be deaf to their false words. Old Uncle Night is not an evil god, just as death is not an evil thing. Life and Death are two sides of the same coin. Keep your faith strong, and we will meet again in the Uncle's hall.

Vincenzo Salvatore

Grandfather, bless me to this sunrise.
Grandfather, bless me to this sunset.
Bless, O bless, God of Shadows
Each hour and stride of my journey.
    May my summers and winters be short.
    May my springs be mild,
    And autumn reaping, plentiful.

Grandfather, bless this pathway on which I go.
Grandfather, bless the earth beneath my sole.
Bless, O bless, and give me your strength.
O God of Shadows, bless my travel and rest.
    May my summers and winters be short.
    May my springs be mild,
    And autumn reaping, plentiful.

ONE

Carmine D'Mario sat watching the Daemyn hounds at the edge of the campsite. He loved how their strong and agile bodies moved. Sleek and black, Daemyn hounds were the ultimate hunters. Some claimed the Draqon breeds were greater hunters, but Carmine disagreed; Draqons were the greatest warriors – a different thing altogether. Daemyn hounds existed for only one purpose, to hunt and kill whatever their summoner sent them after.

Nicco had also loved Daemyn hounds. Just before they had ridden to meet the others for the picnic, Nicco couldn't stop talking about how when the Brotherhood rose to Zenith he would always have a pack ready to devour anyone who displeased him. Now he would have no pack, now or ever, and it was all Carmine's fault. He had predicted every detail of the attack except Julianna. Khellan and the Morigahnti had reacted just the way he expected, and the other girls had transformed into so many hens when the fox comes calling at the coop. Not Julianna. She was a fox in disguise, possessing some reserve of strength. If only the higher ranking Adepts had listened to Carmine's instincts and attacked with the hounds first, Nicco would still be alive.

Trying to ease his spirit, Carmine pictured Nicco now in the Uncle's hall, feasting on the finest food, served by those whose souls had been punished by the Rite of Undoing. Nicco would have the most beautiful women whenever he wanted. If he grew tired of one, Old Uncle Night's servants would find another more to his liking. Even with these comforts, Carmine could not bring himself to feel any joy at his brother's passing. Nicco was gone, and Carmine missed him.

His only joy, though hollow, was in knowing that the vile whore had a Daemyn spawn growing in her belly at this very moment. It wasn't a harsh enough punishment to satisfy Carmine, but it would have to do for now. Once the Brotherhood rose to Zenith, he would find Julianna again. Then she would spend the rest of her life as a brood mare, forever pregnant with Daemyn spawn. Occasionally, Carmine might allow her to believe that her torment had ended, but then he'd return and smash that hope. After a lifetime of suffering at his hand, Carmine might consider that restitution for Nicco's early death.

Taking his eyes away from the hounds, Carmine made sure camp was being set up properly. Even in his heartache, he still had duties to perform. And a true Adept of Old Uncle Night did not show grief at the death of a loved one. Death was a necessary part of the cycle of Life, Death, and Rebirth. All creatures must play out their appointed role, then pass through the cycle again, but understanding that did not still the ache in Carmine's chest.

Four Nightbrothers cared for the horses, brushing down and watering both the riding animals and the draft horses used to pull the wagon carrying the food and gear. Three Brothers staked out a perimeter. Two gathered firewood, while one stood guard over the girls, Sylvie and Colette, who were making dinner. Six erected a large pavilion for Carmine's master. Another four, these also in pairs, busied themselves with pitching the small tents shared by the rest of the Brothers. Normally they would have slept under the open sky, but it looked as though a storm was coming in from the east.

It wasn't compassion that caused Carmine's current teacher, Hardin Thorinson of House Swaenmarch, to order the tents pitched. He didn't want the men using the rain as an excuse for inept performance of their duties. Hardin was a stern taskmaster who required every aspect of life to adhere to his exact specifications. According to Hardin, this attention to every detail, no matter how miniscule, helped maintain that same precision when bargaining with Daemyns. Carmine saw no fault in this logic and followed Hardin's footsteps by putting this philosophy into practice in his own life. Much of the time that meant making sure the rank and file Brothers followed Hardin's orders to the letter. If they failed, the Brothers rarely felt Hardin's wrath. That cold anger always focused on Carmine, and the punishments were far from pleasant.

Turning his mind away from any potential punishments, Carmine looked over at the girls again. Julianna's maid, Colette, had transitioned nicely into a serving girl for the men. However, Countess Sylvie Raelle remained full of the overconfident pride the young nobility of any land seemed to share.

As if she felt Carmine's eyes on her, Sylvie turned to look at him. Her lips began to curl, but she stopped the movement and smoothed her face. Yesterday she'd learned to keep her face and words respectful. The Brothers refused to tolerate her spoiled behavior, and she sported a dark bruise on her left cheek for her attitude.

Sylvie's eyes tightened around the outside edges as she glared at him. The ice-blue of her eyes, so bright that it was still easily seen in the fading light of dusk, looked like the clear sky of winter just after a blizzard. Carmine had seen such a sky once in the northern lands of House Swaenmarch. After he had been trapped indoors for three days, the blizzard finally blew itself out, and Carmine went outside wrapped in furs against the cold. The sky that morning was a crisper blue than he'd ever seen in the southern lands of House Floraen, but it also held defiance stretching from one horizon to the other that said, *You shall never conquer me.* Sylvie's eyes were the same color.

It wasn't the first time he'd received that hateful glare. Several times he'd approached her about becoming his woman. Where Sylvie was not yet a woman by Komati custom, her sixteen years barely made her an adult in the Kingdom of the Sun. And sixteen was not really that far from his own age of twenty-one, the age of majority among the Komati. She was pretty, despite her bruised cheek. Carmine could see the beauty she would become when he closed his eyes and set his imagination adrift. There had been an attraction between them over the past two years. He called attention to that frequently as they rode. He'd argued that they might develop enough passion to lead to marriage. His peculiar station in Kingdom precedence allowed him a freedom in choosing a wife that was unknown to most Kingdom High Blood. Each time he broached the subject, Sylvie fixed him with that scornful glare.

"Carmine!" a voice barked from the other side of the camp.

Master Hardin's call pulled Carmine from his daydreams. It also pulled Sylvie from her defiance, and she returned to work. Their guard, Jorgen, a commoner from House Swaenmarch, should have been paying attention to the girls. However, he stood sharpening a knife. Obviously, that task was far more important than watching the prisoners.

Drawing his rapier, Carmine veered behind Jorgen and gave his backside a quick jab. Yelping, Jorgen spun, murder in his eyes. Finding Carmine gazing back at him, Jorgen's eyes grew wide.

"No dinner for you this night," Carmine said. "And a double watch."

"Yes, Adept." Jorgen bowed. "Thank you."

Carmine sensed the gratitude was genuine. Although strict, he tried to make any punishment fit the offense. This contrasted with Hardin's leadership, who was prone to cruel punishments for the smallest incidents. The Brothers might not like Carmine, but they hated Hardin, and the younger Adept felt he'd earned their respect.

He could live with respect.

He often laughed over the invulnerability that most Adepts felt while wearing their mantles. He had no such delusions. A day was coming when Hardin would push Carmine too far. When the confrontation came, Carmine wanted the Brothers to stand behind him.

Clapping Jorgen on the shoulder, Carmine said, "Don't thank me too loudly. Adept Hardin might hear you. You're not supposed to look relieved by a punishment."

Jorgen nodded. His cheeks sank, but there was nothing hiding the smile in his eyes when he said, "*Thankful?* For no food and little sleep after the hard ride we've had today. I'll be lucky to stay in my saddle tomorrow."

"See that you do," Carmine said, "else wise, you'll be walking the next day."

"Yes, Adept Carmine."

Before turning toward Hardin's pavilion, Carmine looked at Sylvie. She'd been shooting glances at him during the interchange with Jorgen. He smiled. It was his mother's smile, full of warmth and caring. He'd practiced that smile for countless hours in front of a mirror. More than one maiden had lost her resolve, and subsequently her virtue, to that practiced expression. Sylvie's older sister had been one of those maids, and less than a month ago at that.

"I can free you from this," Carmine said, gesturing at the pots, food, and fire.

"At what cost, *Marquis* D'Mario?" Sylvie spoke his title as though it were a profanity.

He knew that she knew what he wanted. She was a countess by birth and spoke frequently of marrying higher, a duke at the very least, perhaps even a prince. Ever since his father's people had conquered hers, the Komati no longer had kings or emperors.

"Only your heart and your love," Carmine replied, refusing to let her goad him.

"You could at least use different words to woo me than you did my sister." Though her tone was the essence of civility, she spoke through clenched teeth. "It's like you have a script for this."

Jorgen snorted a laugh. Carmine turned his head and glared at the Brother, whose face reddened. Clapping Jorgen on the shoulder again, Carmine forced a chuckle.

"Let her scoff. It will only serve to continue her servitude to you and the others. Good evening, Countess Raelle." This last he said with a great bow.

So, Perrine had told Sylvie. That explained much. It would also make it that much sweeter when Sylvie finally gave herself to him. Carmine felt her eyes on his back as he strode toward Hardin's tent. Before he'd taken five steps, Jorgen barked at her to get back to work.

When Carmine approached the pavilion, the Brothers on guard saluted.

The furnishings were not as lavish as a palace, though Hardin did demand a certain level of comfort. The pavilion had a canvas floor covered with fine carpets. There was a table with two chairs, with one table setting waiting for the girls to finish cooking. A bottle of wine was already open with a crystal goblet next to it, half-full. To the right was Hardin's bedroom, containing a bed with a feather mattress. All of the furniture was collapsible and carried in the wagon.

Turning left, Carmine entered the room that Hardin used for his observances to Old Uncle Night.

Hardin stood before a pedestal of silver about two arms high, supporting a circle of the same metal one arm across, with a variety of gems worked into both the circle and stand. Each of those gems shone with an inner light. Multicolored smoke swirled within the circle. The object was an artifact used by the faith Hardin publicly claimed. To those outside the Brotherhood of the Night, Hardin was an Adept of Aunt Moon, goddess of House Swaenmarch.

The Brotherhood were the only ones to realize that the gifts of all the gods were open to those who understood the god's divine language and knew the proper steps of speaking miracles, performing rituals, or creating artifacts. Any Adept from other Houses that discovered this always met with unfortunate accidents, insuring the Brotherhood of the Night were the only ones who knew this secret.

"You took your time," Hardin said.

"One of the Brothers watching the girls was growing lax," Carmine replied. "I took it upon myself to insure that it did not happen again."

Hardin grunted and gave one quick nod of his head. The wisps of gray hair on the sides of his head waved as he made the gesture. Those wisps were the only hair he had. Although Hardin was in his early thirties, he looked ready to leave life behind. He'd traded his youth to a Daemyn. Now he looked as frail as his thinning hair. Carmine had yet to learn what Hardin had received in that bargain.

"I am about to contact the First Adept," Hardin answered. "I thought you might like to be present for the communication."

"Thank you, Master," Carmine said.

"I have already begun the ritual," Hardin said. "We are waiting for the First Adept to grant us an audience."

Of course he had started the ritual. One of Carmine's greatest annoyances about serving Hardin was the other Adept's need to constantly state the obvious, as if he felt Carmine possessed an infantile mind that needed constant coddling.

After a few minutes, Hardin started grumbling under his breath. Carmine couldn't make out most of the words, but then one word came out clearly.

"Octavio." Hardin actually spoke the First Adept's name out loud.

Carmine kept his face still. It was forbidden to speak the First Adept's name while acting as a member the Brotherhood of the Night. If Harden suspected that Carmine had heard him, Carmine could count himself dead within the next day. It wouldn't be murder, but one of the many *accidents* that happened while traveling hard.

The smoke contained within the silver circle gathered, and the First Adept's face took form out of the smoke. His features were muted, but there was no mistaking the weight of his strong gaze. The First Adept looked from Hardin to Carmine. He studied them, looking for something in their eyes, as if he could ferret out their secrets with his gaze alone. There was nothing pleasant in his scrutiny.

"Is something amiss?" Hardin asked.

"Yes," the First Adept said. "Although your mission to kill the Lord Morigahn was not a complete disaster, you and Roark butchered the task."

"First Adept," Hardin said, "we made sure that…"

"Stop." The First Adept's voice snapped like a cracked whip. Hardin flinched as if struck. "You made sure of nothing. Somehow, Julianna Taraen summoned an avatar of Grandfather Shadow to save her. Roark is dead, as are all the Brothers who served him. The avatar marked her as the new Lord Morigahn and summoned a guardian for her. The guardian's name is Faelin vara'Traejyn."

Carmine gasped, both in outrage that Julianna had escaped her fate and at hearing Faelin was still alive.

"I'm as surprised as you are," the First Adept said. "The Kingdom thought all the Traejyn family dead. I will be speaking to several High Blood of my House over this." There was an ominous finality in that remark. "I don't understand how the girl managed to summon an avatar, but it is done. Leaving saved your lives, and that is a blessing. However, your task remains incomplete. Your prey rides hard to the northwest. You still have a chance to catch them. When you do, kill them both."

"First Adept?" Carmine said, keeping his eyes downcast. One did not normally address the First Adept before he acknowledged you.

"Yes, Carmine?"

"I had no knowledge of Julianna's faith," Carmine said.

"I believe you," the First Adept replied. "I know that you lie to me. We serve the God of Lies. However, you wouldn't keep that from either Hardin or me."

"Yes, First Adept." That was half a lie. Carmine wouldn't keep information like that from the First Adept, but he would keep it from Hardin, for the right reasons.

"And I am sorry for Nicco," the First Adept said. "I was very fond of him."

"Thank you, First Adept." Though Carmine felt anything but thanks. Hearing Nicco's name was like drinking poorly aged Aernacht whiskey; it burned from neck to navel.

"Some of our order might tell you that showing any emotion for your loss is a sign of weakness. They would have you believe that the sooner death comes, the better, for that means the Uncle will embrace you. Do not believe these things, Carmine. Death can only be appreciated by celebrating life, and one of the ways to celebrate life is to mourn the passing of those we love. I give you my full leave to shed every tear you must in order to bless your brother's passing. I will mention Nicco tonight when I speak at the service. He will be well remembered."

"Thank you, First Adept," Carmine said, choking back his tears. He refused to cry before Hardin. There was time for tears after he'd gone to bed.

The First Adept's image turned to Hardin. "Catch them and fix this. Do not contact me again until you have done so."

"Yes, First Adept," Hardin said.

The smoke in the circle dissipated, and the first Adept was gone.

Hardin turned to Carmine. "We leave at first light. They have a day and a half on us. I mean to catch them within the week. The last thing we need is for them to join with other Morigahnti."

"Yes, Master." Carmine bowed and left the pavilion.

None of the Brothers would be pleased. They were expecting to return to their homes and families. Even though they were all devout, they had lives outside the Brotherhood. Over the next few days they would all be discussing the lies they would have to tell to explain their delayed return.

Carmine moved through the camp, telling the Brothers of their early departure. They hid their disappointment well. He tried to reassure them, explaining that while Hardin would never consider their feelings, Carmine appreciated their sacrifice and would remember them to the First Adept when the Brotherhood took the Zenith away from House Floraen. While his words were eloquent, his voice sounded hollow even to his own ears. Now that Carmine discovered that he was permitted to mourn, his grief threatened to overwhelm him.

As he passed the girls, Sylvie muttered under her breath. He couldn't make out the words, but understood her condescending tone all too well.

Carmine's lips pulled back in a snarl, and all the muscles in the back of his neck and shoulders tightened. He spun and fixed his gaze on Sylvie. Her sideways smirk dissolved as she took a step away from him. They stood, locked in each other's gaze. Carmine wanted to scream some retort, but his rage took all his words away.

Finally, Sylvie turned away and returned to her work.

Carmine retreated to his tent and managed to keep the tears from flowing until he made it inside. He buried his face in his pillow as the sobs started. Time lost all meaning as he wept in grief for Nicco.

Later, after he regained some semblance of self-control, Carmine rolled over and stared at the ceiling of his tent. Pushing thoughts of Nicco out of his mind, Carmine forced himself back to the present. The First Adept was right. The best way for Carmine to honor Nicco's death was to celebrate life.

At the moment, he needed to discern the First Adept's reasons for pairing him with Hardin Thorinson. The only certainty was that it was not a true master and disciple relationship. The First Adept was Carmine's true master although he frequently sent Carmine to study with other Adepts within the Brotherhood. Sometimes he was convinced that the First Adept sent him to learn what *not* to do as often as what to do.

Thunder roared in the distance, and Carmine rolled onto his side. As sleep overcame him, his thoughts wandered between memories of Nicco and wondering what lessons he was supposed to learn from Hardin.

TWO

Julianna's eyes snapped open. Her breath came in ragged sobs as she tried to push the nightmare aside and ignored the throbbing in her right cheek. She had tried to nap when Faelin had stopped to rest the horses and hunt for food, for all the good that did her.

She should have known better.

Resting was impossible for her. Every time she closed her eyes she saw either Khellan swinging from the tree or the Daemyn's glowing eyes. This time those visions had waited until she was asleep, and in her dreams Julianna dreamt of the Daemyn's eyes looking out of Khellan's face while they both raped her.

As Julianna struggled to drive the nightmare away, the strange language and knowledge Grandfather Shadow had placed in her mind threatened to overwhelm her. She pushed her palms against her head, trying to squeeze the interloping words and visions away. With slow steady breaths, the visions of Khellan and the Daemyn's eyes faded. The words didn't. It was like the morning after a feast or a ball when she woke with the best songs always at the front of her memory. Only she never remembered all of the songs, just enough that they bled together, making an unpleasant jumble of words that refused to go away.

This was far worse.

At least she understood the songs. She could comprehend the words dancing just behind her eyes if she concentrated on them, but that took too much effort. And most of those words told her things she'd rather not know. Some told her how to make a man's shadow skin him alive, how to summon lighting and thunder to devastate her enemies, and other, even more horrid, things.

Rolling to a sitting position, Julianna hugged her arms around her shoulders, trying to warm herself from a chill that had nothing to do with the air around her. The late afternoon was fairly warm, just like it had been yesterday and the day before for her birthday picnic.

Thinking of the others made Julianna shiver. Maybe the dead were the lucky ones. The Brotherhood of the Night had carried off Colette, Sophya, and Perrine's younger sister, Sylvie. Were any of them still alive? If they were, had they been offered over to Daemyns for breeding? She forced the thoughts away. Dwelling on her friends' fate would do nothing but work Julianna into a frenzy of worry and guilt.

Faelin was still gone, presumably to gather food in order to help make what he'd scavenged last longer. Julianna had mixed feelings about his return to her life, and so she'd said nothing to him. However, she couldn't stay silent forever, and that meant dealing with even more harsh truths.

Reaching into the saddlebags, Julianna took an apple and stood. She walked to where Faelin had tethered the horses to graze.

Julianna called out softly, "Vendyr."

Vendyr came away from the other horses.

Julianna waited for Vendyr to approach before offering the apple. If she got too close with the fruit, all the horses might come searching for treats. Once Vendyr discovered the apple, he tickled Julianna's fingers with his lips. Julianna opened her hand and gave the apple over. Vendyr chomped happily, rubbing his nose into Julianna's shoulder as he did. Julianna, in turn, wrapped her arms around Vendyr's muzzle and drew in a deep breath. The musky scent of him filled her nose.

Vendyr finished the apple and started sniffing for another.

"*Minas ankae—.*" She had started to say, *I'm sorry. I don't have another apple*, but that strange language pushed its way into her speech. Forcing words that should have been as familiar as breathing through her lips, she said, "What am I going to do, Vendyr?"

Vendyr just kept searching for a second apple. Julianna couldn't help but smile at his tenacity. Even though Vendyr couldn't make these current troubles better, he provided a solace and a strong foundation.

"Julianna?" Faelin said from behind her.

She started a bit. She hadn't heard him approach. Vendyr danced away from her sudden movement.

Julianna turned. Faelin really hadn't changed in five years. He was still dark and handsome, without being pretty or desirable.

"Are you alright?" Faelin asked.

Julianna concentrated, making sure she spoke in her normal language. "Yesterday the man I loved was hung before my eyes, I was nearly raped," she intentionally left out, *by a Daemyn*, "a god rescued me, that same god cut my face with a red-hot knife, I found out that you are alive, and ever since I've been fighting to stay awake to keep the nightmares away. I think I'm doing quite well, considering."

Speaking of those things brought the memories fresh to her mind. Turning away from Faelin, she buried her face into Vendyr's neck and choked back her tears. She had shed enough tears already. Somehow she would find her vengeance, just as she had been promised.

"Don't shut me out, Julianna," Faelin said. "I'm still your friend."

"What do you know of friendship?" She spun on him. "You let us all believe you were dead. We grieved for you."

"*Kostota*," Faelin whispered.

Julianna's grasped her mother's knife tucked into her belt. She recalled some of the memories that came before Grandfather Shadow filled her mind. Her parents had taught her some words in *Galad'laman. Kostota* could mean debt, obligation, or revenge. No matter how one viewed *kostota*, it must be repaid, whether for good or for ill.

"I'm sorry for leaving," Faelin said. "It was wrong to let you all think I was dead, but it couldn't be helped. I can only try to make it right now that I'm back."

"You wish to meet your *kostota*?" Julianna asked.

Faelin nodded.

"Why did you come back now? It's awfully convenient that you appeared right when I needed someone most."

Faelin took a deep breath, looked into the sky, and let the breath out. He was keeping something from her, thinking that he was doing her some good, or protecting her in some way, just like when they were younger.

"I am in no mood for secrets, Faelin vara'Traejyn," Julianna said. "I have very little trust for anyone right now."

"Yes, my lady," Faelin said. Then he added, barely above a whisper. "Shadows lie to their enemies, not to each other."

Again, words came unbidden into her mind. *The hunter does not lie down with his prey.* It was Grandfather Shadow's Fifth Law.

Faelin bent to one knee. He drew his sword, put the tip on the ground, and gripped the hilt with both hands.

"I, Faelin vara'Traejyn, natural son of Raelian Tsieskas'Traejyn, swear to serve the Lord Morigahn, Julianna Kolmonen'Taraen, first chosen of Grandfather Shadow with my life's blood and breath. I am a true-blooded child of Koma and shall serve with no expectation of reward, payment, or recompense. I live and die by the will of Grandfather Shadow and the Lord Morigahn."

Julianna's breath quickened, and her hands started trembling. She looked away, first at the horses and then to the sky. How could he mock her like this?

With a deep breath, she stilled herself and looked back at Faelin. He still knelt there, looking expectant. Julianna took two steps, placing herself right in front of Faelin. She looked down at him, and he returned the gaze.

"Why are you doing this?" she demanded.

"You are the Lord Morigahn," Faelin said, "as Khellan was before you. I didn't know to be here. I was traveling through Heidenmarch. When I woke, I found myself near you. Grandfather Shadow sent me to protect you."

Julianna slapped him.

The instant she struck Faelin, pain flared down the right side of her face. She felt the hot blade cutting down her forehead, missing her eye, and continuing down her cheek all the way to her chin. The god had cut her only a day ago, but the pain had faded shortly after and remained gone until now. Her vision blackened, and she dropped to the earth. A pair of cold eyes regarded her in the darkness of her mind.

This behavior ill becomes the Lord Morigahn, a voice sounded in her mind.

As the disapproval sounded in Julianna's mind, the pain stopped. It went away just as it had come, suddenly, without any warning. But even though the physical hurt was gone, the memory remained. She sat up, gasping for breath.

"No," she said, barely louder than a whisper. "I will not do this. I will not be this." She turned her face to the heavens and shouted. "I *cannot* be this!" She dropped her chin to her chest. "Please, find someone else."

You have already agreed and stepped upon the path, the voice said, barely a whisper at the back of her mind. Then, it was gone.

Thunder rumbled in the distance.

"There is no one else," Faelin groaned.

She turned to him. Faelin sat cross-legged, rubbing his face where she'd struck him. Tears rolled down his cheeks. As children, he'd kept his emotions in tight control. His father thought excessive emotions were a weakness, and Faelin spent most of his youth trying to win his father's approval. Faelin's only outlet for his feelings had been the times he and Julianna were alone.

"How do you know?" Julianna asked. "How can you be sure that I am the only one who can do this?"

"You can't pass it on, Julianna. Anyone worthy of the title would not take it from you."

"Why not?"

"You are the first Lord Morigahn marked by Grandfather Shadow in a thousand years. You are his first chosen, his high priest. All of those who are faithful to him will look to you for guidance. Some will even want you to lead a Komati rebellion."

Comprehension hit Julianna like a biting wind. Everything she had been taught about the gods and religion was wrong. More than that came the realization that Grandfather Shadow had marked her for death. It was only a matter of time before the Kingdom discovered her. Then she would be executed for breaking the Kingdom's highest law. Only the

High Blood of the four Great Houses worshiped the greater gods. Anyone within their conquered lands found worshipping above their station was sentenced to the Ritual of Undoing, a public execution ceremony that damned the offender's soul to the Dark Realm of the Godless Dead. Bearing a Daemyn's child would be better than that. Once that horror was over, she would eventually die and pass through the cycle of Life, Death, and Rebirth, forgetting the horrors of this life.

Now she understood Faelin's tears.

He looked at her with concern in his eyes. She remembered that look.

"I don't want to talk about it," Julianna said, as Faelin opened his mouth.

He paused for a moment, and then said, "I understand, but there is something I have to ask you about. Just one thing, and I'll leave it be. If it weren't important, I wouldn't ask."

She drew in a deep breath. The last thing she wanted right now was to think about it in any way, and she thought she knew what he was going to ask her about. It was something that he needed to know, and he deserved an answer no matter how much Julianna wished she could pretend none of it had happened.

"Alright," she said, bracing herself.

"While you were sleeping last night, you muttered something about a betrayer," Faelin said. "Did someone betray you, or perhaps Khellan?"

That was not the question she expected, not the question she had prepared for. Caught by surprise, her breath caught in her throat as the shock and fear returned.

"Yes," she whispered.

"Who?"

"Carmine and Nicco D'Mario." She felt vile and unclean speaking their names.

"Our friends Carmine and Nicco?" Faelin asked.

"They are friends to no one," Julianna snapped. "They worship Old Uncle Night. They're the reason Khellan is dead."

Faelin's face hardened.

Khellan was one of the few Komati nobles who accepted Faelin as a man in his own right, rather than as his father's mistake. Faelin was a bastard, sired by a noble father on a peasant girl. He spent all of his life trying to live down a shame that was no fault of his own.

Carmine, on the other side of the coin, was much like Faelin. He was one of those poor products of a union between the conqueror and the conquered. His father was High Blood of House Floraen, and his mother a Komati noble of the Raelle family. The Raelle family shared the same house as Faelin's family, Traejyn. In some ways, Carmine was an even greater social pariah than Faelin. Faelin was just a bastard. Carmine was a half-breed with no real place in either society.

"*Kostota*," Faelin said. "We will find a way to make them pay."

"We can have *kostota* with Carmine," Julianna replied. "It's too late for Nicco."

"Why?"

Julianna allowed herself a grim smile. "I killed him."

"I had a reason for asking you about betrayal," Faelin said. "Soon, the Morigahnti will come looking for you. The power they give you might be intoxicating, but you must not let it rule you, and you must always keep your guard up around them. Some of them may want to betray you."

"I'm the high priest. Why wouldn't they be loyal to me?"

"Just because someone is a Morigahnti doesn't mean they hold to the old traditions. If the Morigahnti managed to stop their squabbling, they might unite Koma to successfully rebel against the Kingdom. It has almost happened a few times in the past, but has always failed because someone high in the Morigahnti ranks has betrayed the Lord Morigahn. Once, the Lord Morigahn betrayed all Koma. That's how Koma fell to the Kingdom of the Sun."

"Why?"

"Because all men can be corrupted by power. It is much the same with Kingdom Adepts. More and more, being a man or woman of faith in any land becomes more about mortal politics and less about cultivating the small spark of divinity in the human soul."

"Where did you learn all this?" Julianna asked.

"In my five years of traveling," Faelin replied, "I saw the evils of the world firsthand." He turned toward the horses. "We've been here long enough. We can talk more on the move."

They fell silent as they saddled the horses. Even when she hadn't been speaking to Faelin, she'd made it known that she could saddle and tack Vendyr. The familiar process helped calm her. As they mounted and rode, Julianna found herself dwelling on Faelin's words about the Morigahnti. Grandfather Shadow wanted her to lead these people? It seemed that some of them might not be too welcoming. Perhaps Grandfather Shadow enjoyed the irony of her, an unbeliever, leading his army of people who claimed to be believers, yet most of whom were not. Yet, was she really an unbeliever? Mother and Father had believed, before they were killed. Julianna even remembered times where Father had preached to the household. The memories still felt like they belonged to some other person, but at one point, Julianna had been part of a community that remembered the truth.

In the distance, thunder roared, low and angry. The word *ruth* came unbidden into her mind. It was Grandfather Shadow's word for thunder, but it could also mean raw, unbridled power, or even anger and rage. As she thought of the ways various words in *Galad'laman* changed definition depending upon context, each of those phrases struggled with each other for her attention. The knowledge of that language was her power, her *ruth*, only she didn't know how to harness or control it yet.

"Are you—?" Faelin started.

Julianna held up her hand. She closed her eyes and focused. Something in all those various words had pulled at her, something that might have an answer for her. She needed to get those mostly out of the front her mind in order to determine what it was.

"*Kostota*?" That wasn't it. "*Kraestu*?" No. "*Karkota*?" Julianna felt as though she was getting further from what she wanted.

She shook her head.

This was the wrong way to go about it. She could keep thinking of words in *Galad'laman*, and it would take her forever. It was something Faelin had said, or maybe that he'd asked. He'd asked her about something she'd said in her sleep.

"*Kavala*," Julianna said.

"What?" Faelin asked. "I am—"

"Not you," Julianna said. "*Carmine un aen kavala.* I wouldn't have used 'betrayer' in my sleep. I would have spoken of *kavala.* You speak *Galad'laman.*"

Faelin nodded.

"Where did you learn it?"

"My family. We all worshipped Grandfather Shadow. The House Floraen Inquisitors killed them all."

They rode in silence for a time. Julianna suspected Faelin was thinking of his family, as she was thinking of hers, but her memories of that time were still clouded. More of her thoughts were about *Galad'laman*. If Faelin knew the language, perhaps he could tell her how to command its power.

THREE

A wet wind, cold enough to bite straight to the bone, howled in the night. Rain pattered against the wagon. Sylvie shivered, her teeth chattered, and no matter how she tried, she could not stay warm even with her two blankets wrapped around her. At least she and Julianna's maid had been allowed to sleep underneath the wagon, which offered some small protection from the rain and wind. Sylvie glared at the shadowy lump of the maid, also shivering in her two blankets. The girl should have at the very least offered Sylvie one of the blankets; the girl was, after all, only a servant, while Sylvie was a countess. But it seemed proper decorum had been forgotten the moment the two had been taken prisoner by the Brotherhood of the Night.

Deciding the rain had calmed as much as it was ever going to, Sylvie crawled out of her blankets. She tucked them underneath the axel to keep them from blowing into the mud. She shed her overdress and put it next to the blankets.

"What are you doing, my lady?" The maid whispered.

Sylvie fixed the servant with her most practiced look of disdain.

"Your Excellency," Sylvie corrected. "Not that it is any of your concern, but I'm going to make myself a little more comfortable."

"Please, my lady, uh, Your Excellency. Don't do anything to get us punished."

"You are no one to command me," Sylvie said, and crawled out from under the wagon.

The only thing Sylvie's plan might earn her was a little bit of momentary humiliation, but it was time to stop living like a peasant. If that meant sharing a bed with a man she could barely stomach, so be it. She would rather suffer that indignity than spend one more day under the illusion that she and the maid were in any way equal.

Once out from underneath the wagon, the wind bit with an even greater chill, but Sylvie had expected it and steeled herself against it. Like many ladies at court, she had practiced the art of appearing unperturbed in the face of humiliation and great discomfort. She allowed herself to shiver and her teeth to chatter only as much as needed to gain sympathy. The thin material of her chemise rubbed against her hardening nipples. Carmine would like that. Even though she had seen only sixteen winters, she knew what men wanted and what they liked to see. She'd seen her father's friends leering at her alongside their sons.

"What are you about?"

Startled, Sylvie turned around. Jorgen stood not five paces away. His eyes bore into hers for a moment, and then he lowered his gaze. This attention nauseated and excited Sylvie. She pulled her shoulder blades together, helping to enhance her small bosom.

"I'm going to entertain Adept Carmine D'Mario," Sylvie said.

Jorgen sucked in a deep breath through his nose as he chewed on his lower lip. Sylvie saw the war waging in his mind. Adept Harden had commanded the men not to touch Sylvie or Colette. That command might be all well and good while the girls were fully dressed during the light of day, but being alone in the night with a girl in only her small clothes, Jorgen's eyes shone with hungry temptation.

"I'll not have you wandering the camp on my watch," Jorgen said. "Get back under that wagon."

Apparently his good sense won out over his desire.

"I don't think you'll be punished for letting me go to Adept Carmine. In fact, he might even reward you." She covered the distance between then. "And so would I."

Jorgen pulled back a bit. "You would lay with me?"

Sylvie smiled her most flirtatious smile. "Don't be silly. Carmine would punish us both for that. But there are *other* ways for me to pleasure you."

"How?" Jorgen looked suspicious now.

"I have hands." Sylvie leaned toward him, and said in a low, conspire-atorial whisper, "and if you're very nice to me, I have a mouth."

In truth, she found the idea vile, and choked down the urge to vomit, but she'd heard her sister talking about it once. It might well be the most disgusting thing in the world, but if it got her out from under the wagon, Sylvie would do it. She might not be very ladylike right now, but once she escaped and told Father everything, he would go directly to the Kingdom Governor, Duke Octavio Salvatore. Then everyone here would die, and whatever she had to do to survive until then would die with them.

Jorgen grinned. "Well then, let's put those hands to better use than cooking."

He took her wrist and led her to a spot where the wagon blocked most of the camp from view. As he pulled at his belt, Sylvie swore she would please Carmine enough tonight that she wouldn't have to endure this again. After tonight, Carmine would take her straight into his bed.

FOUR

It was well into the early hours of the morning when Carmine heard hushed voices outside his tent. Even though the weather had settled, he could not make out the words. Reaching under his pillow, Carmine grabbed the forearm bone of a man long dead. The bone had been hollowed out and was filled with a powder blessed with the divinity of Old Uncle Night. The powder would paralyze any who inhaled it. If some interloper was going to sneak into his tent, Carmine wanted to know who and why before they died

The tent flap opened. A small, shadowed figure crawled through the opening. He was about to blow the powder out when the invader spoke.

"Carmine?" Sylvie asked. "Are you awake?"

Carmine removed the bone from his lips. "What do you want?"

She crawled toward him. In the dim light he saw her hair plastered to her face from the rain, her eyes still holding that hard edge of hate.

"I've been thinking about my situation," she said. "You're right. I don't want to suffer through this any longer."

She kissed him. Her lips were like icicles. The chill of the wind and rain outside clung to her. After a moment, Carmine grew bold and went to deepen the kiss. Sylvie let him put his tongue in her mouth for a moment, and then she sucked on his lower lip. His toes tingled.

When the kiss ended, she pulled her shift over her head and knelt naked before him. With each movement, the hatred in her eyes grew. Carmine smiled, but he could not allow Sylvie to believe charms would win him that easily. She crawled forward and lay down on him.

"Just a moment," Carmine said, rolling out from under her.

"What is it?"

He collected her discarded shift and held it out to her. "You dropped something."

Sylvie's mouth hung open. Carmine could just imagine the torrent of confusion warring in her head.

"But," Sylvie started.

"Go back to bed, Excellency," Carmine said. "I want to be alone."

Sylvie's lower lip quivered. Even in the dark of the tent, Carmine saw her eyes welling with tears. She wriggled back into her shift, a sight Carmine enjoyed very much. Once she was dressed again, Sylvie fled.

The smoldering fire in Carmine's groin screamed at him to call her, to summon her back. Taking her tonight could relieve him in so many ways beyond simply slaking his lust. However, to do so would give her the power, put her in control. If he allowed that, the battle between them would never end. Just as with dealing with Adept Hardin and learning whatever lesson the First Adept intended, Carmine must be patient.

Carmine lay back down and closed his eyes. The vision of Sylvie's body filled his mind, especially her pert breasts. His heartbeat and breath quickened as he used that vision to pleasure himself to sleep.

FIVE

Dawn had come, such as it was with the storm clouds overhead. Julianna and Faelin had been traveling an hour already. The warmth that always preceded the first storm of autumn had gone. The storm had lessened to a steady drizzle and the wind had receded so that the raindrops no longer stung Julianna's face, but her clothes and hair still clung to her skin.

Faelin rode next to her. He'd spent most of their time this morning trying to explain how to focus the power of Grandfather Shadow's divine language through the *Galad'fana* in order to speak miracles. No matter how hard she tried, Julianna couldn't seem to take the words and get them to *do* something.

"What am I doing wrong?" Julianna asked through chattering teeth.

"First, you're not pronouncing the words correctly," Faelin said. "Second, you don't *want* the miracles to happen."

"Yes I do," Julianna retorted. "If I'm going to have this other language filling my mind, I want to be able to do something with it. Grandfather Shadow cursed me with this power. The least he could have done was make it easier to use."

Faelin shook his head and sighed. "You'll never be able to speak miracles as long as you think of them as a curse. You must believe this is a gift."

"How can I think of it as a gift when I didn't want it?"

"Do you remember when Eddryck gave you your first real kiss?" Faelin asked.

"Yes." Julianna's face grew warm.

Eddryck had been Faelin's older half-brother. He had kissed her at a spring ball when she was fourteen. A group of young lords and ladies had gone off to play parlor games. They'd decided to play Wink, a game where the ladies sat in chairs with the gentlemen behind them. One of the chairs was empty, and the gentleman behind that chair would wink at one of the ladies. She would then try to escape her chair and move to that gentleman's chair. When she got to his chair, the lady would give him a chaste kiss on the cheek. When Julianna got to Eddryck's chair and went to kiss his cheek, he turned his head and kissed her lips.

"You didn't know you wanted him to kiss you at the time," Faelin said.

"I was furious," Julianna said. "He embarrassed me so much."

"If I remember rightly, you actually liked it," Faelin replied. "You two spent that whole summer sneaking off together."

Though the memories were embarrassing, Julianna welcomed the warmth that came with her spreading blush.

"You have to think of Grandfather Shadow's blessing like that kiss," Faelin said. "Right now you're angry and confused, but someday you'll see it as something wonderful."

"But if your father had caught us, he wouldn't have killed us," Julianna argued. "The Kingdom will."

Faelin snorted a laugh. "My father might not have, but Eddryck's mother would have skinned you both. Eddryck was promised to Princess Pyrras Collaen."

"Of House Aesin?" Julianna gasped. "That cow would have ruined your brother's life."

"Well, he had hoped to convince Father and his mother that even though you were only a duchess, you would be a more politically advantageous marriage for him, and that Braendyn would be a better match for Pyrras."

Julianna couldn't help but smile. She'd enjoyed the time she'd spent with Eddryck, and not just because of the kissing. He was the first man that made her feel like a woman with his compliments, manners, and by how he treated her as an equal, even though he'd been three years her senior and was a prince of his House. She hadn't found another man that made her feel like that until Khellan. Now both were dead, killed by the Kingdom: Khellan by the Brotherhood of the Night, and Eddryck by House Floraen. Was the Kingdom destined to kill all the men she loved?

She pushed thoughts of both her loves aside. The memories of them only served to distract her, and she had to learn how to speak miracles. Her survival depended on learning to master this skill. If she didn't…well, she couldn't think on that distraction either. She simply must succeed.

As they rode, Julianna kept trying and kept failing.

"Why can't we stop?" Julianna asked. "There are too many distractions, and it's hard to concentrate."

"I hardly think your enemies will give you time to prepare yourself," Faelin replied.

"What I really want is to stop being wet," Julianna said. "If Grandfather Shadow holds dominion over storms, why can't he make it so that the rain doesn't fall on his followers?"

"Perhaps you should ask him for that miracle," Faelin replied.

"Now that *would* be a gift," Julianna said.

She took a deep breath and turned her head to the sky. She felt where the *Galad'fana* touched her head and reached with her mind for the divine power bound into the cloth. Gods and goddesses, she wanted a reprieve from the cold. Julianna's desire melded into the Veil of Shadows, and she grasped the dominion of Storms with her mind. With another deep breath, she made sure she had the words firmly in her mind. She forced her teeth to stop chattering and her lips to stop trembling in the cold. Once Julianna was sure she had complete command of every part of the miracle she wanted, she called to Grandfather Shadow, almost begging.

"Galad'Ysoysa olka hyvae salpa tasti sadela ja kietola ulos herkas mina ja Faelin."

Power surged through her *Galad'fana.* The wind stopped biting her skin, and the rain no longer fell on her.

She had a moment to enjoy this before a wave of exhaustion descended on her. Every muscle seemed to lose some of its strength, and breathing became more difficult. Julianna didn't care. She had spoken a miracle, and Grandfather Shadow had granted it.

She glanced at Faelin. The wind and rain weren't touching him either.

"That was a good miracle," Faelin said, smiling at her.

Julianna returned the smile. Despite the sudden weariness, speaking the miracle had made her feel like she wouldn't be a victim anymore,

more in control of the world around her. The power she'd commanded burned away the last feelings of weakness remaining from the Brotherhood's attack. They would never take her like that again, not when she understood how to bring this power into the world. Wanting even more of that liberating feeling, Julianna sought another target for a second miracle. She saw a small sapling to her right.

Focusing her will through *Galad'laman* and the *Galad'fana*, Julianna drew on the dominions of Shadows and Vengeance, and spoke, "*Tuska.*"

A bolt of dark energy flew from her fingertip. The sapling exploded in a shower of splinters.

Julianna grew even more tired, but she welcomed it. Knowing that she could command the power of Grandfather Shadow filled her with euphoria. Though her body was ready to collapse out of her saddle, she wanted to speak more miracles.

"You have to be careful, Julianna." Faelin's tone carried a hint of reproach. "If you try to do too much too fast, the divine power could burn your body up from the inside out."

"I'll be careful," Julianna replied.

She intended to keep that promise as best she could; she would be as careful as she could. However, she hadn't felt this in control of anything in her life. Now that she understood the process, the phrases and sentencees of *Galad'laman* floating in her mind created a tapestry of miraculous possibilities. Let them come: the Brotherhood of the Night with their foot soldiers in black armor, the House Floraen Inquisitors with their armies of Draqons, and even those traitorous Morigahnti. None of them had the breadth of knowledge that Grandfather Shadow had given her.

Julianna couldn't wait to experiment.

SIX

"Look." Luciano held The Detector out to Santo.

A ball of light and heat, summoned through the divine grace of All Father Sun, floated above them. The glowing orb cast away the gloom of the stormy day and burned the rain to steam above them. Luciano and Santo huddled around The Detector. It had chimed and buzzed, and now Grandfather Shadow's symbol had jumped from a flicker to a steady glow.

"We're getting closer," Santo said. "We should catch up to them by day's end."

"No," Luciano replied. "Not quite, but sometime early tomorrow."

In truth, they could likely overtake whatever was causing three hands to point toward one symbol, if they rode the horses hard and didn't stop to rest. No doubt Santo would leap at that plan, should Luciano give it voice. However, such a course of action would be foolhardy beyond comprehension. Whatever they faced was outside of the experience of any Inquisitor in memory. Both Luciano and Santo would need to have all their wits and faculties about them when they confronted whatever they rode toward.

"We should rest," Luciano said. "Even if only for a few hours."

"And let them get further ahead of us?" Santo's youthful eyes stared greedily toward the west.

Youthful? Luciano had to suppress an indignant snort.

Santo would likely believe such a scornful display meant for him and take offense. Truly, the snort was meant for Luciano himself. How much had nine years as an Inquisitor changed how he looked at the world? Luciano had seen only thirty-nine summers, but he felt ancient next to Santo's thirty-one. Like all Inquisitors, they had each joined the order at thirty and Luciano had vague memories of being as bright and enthusiastic as Santo, but that was before nine years of fighting the worst threats to the Kingdom of the Sun.

"It is likely that our quarry will need to rest at some point also. If they don't, then we best not face them while exhausted."

"Very well," Santo said, his shoulders slumping a little.

"Don't worry. We'll catch them." Luciano put The Detector in the pocket sewn into the inside of his sleeve. He sat straight in his saddle and looked ahead to the west, eyes neither shifting nor blinking. "We are the beacon that guides the righteous beyond the fear and doubt."

Santo snapped upright and spoke the next line of the benediction. "We are the light of Truth in the face of bleak tidings."

"We are the hand of the Sun come to purge darkness from the heart." They both spoke together. "We are the hand of the All Father."

With minds and spirits set to purpose, the two Inquisitors of House Floraen rode to discover the source of this mystery.

SEVEN

Faelin felt someone behind him. No noise had given the person away, and the forest didn't sound any different. The raindrops kept falling. The soft wind continued to blow. Those few birds that enjoyed the rain called back and forth through the trees. Something tingled just behind his navel, behind his nose, and at the back of his knees. It was the oddest sensation Faelin had ever felt, as if all three places on his body were connected to some never-before-tickled nerve.

At the moment, Faelin was only armed with a crossbow and dagger. Hunting with a rapier strapped to his side would be impractical. Hoping the stranger was far enough away for the crossbow to be effective, Faelin spun.

An old man squatted next to a tree, arms propped on his knees. The stranger was dressed in ragged leather and furs, though not in the balanced patterns of the Dosahan to the west, nor did the clothes possess the paint and fringe to commemorate any battles he might have won. His hair and beard were as wild and untamed as his clothing.

For just a moment, Faelin considered loosing the crossbow in his hands, until he saw the man's eyes. Though his hair was dark, the stranger's eyes were the white of fresh fallen snow, and those eyes stared unblinking at Faelin. Even if the quarrel struck true, it would likely prove little more than an annoyance.

"Interesting weaponry you have there." The man's voice came a bit like a growl. "A crossbow and a dirk won't help you much with the people hunting you. What would you have done if I'd been a Daemyn or maybe one of those alchemically-bred Draqon soldiers the Kingdom uses?"

"Crossbow and dirk kill a Draqon just as well as anything else.'

"Perhaps. If you are better than they are." The man sniffed the air. "Something tells me you are not."

Faelin shrugged. "I'd think of something. Though I doubt any of them could sneak up on me as well as you have."

"That is very true," the man said with a chuckle. "But a Daemyn hound could have."

"True enough," Faelin said. "Then I guess I would die."

"At least you have the good sense to know that."

"Once we were like wolves," Faelin said, hoping and dreading that his suspicions of the man were true.

"Our time will come again," the man half-growled in response. "Though I give the greeting as a matter of formality. I hold no belief in it."

"It is my honor to meet you," Faelin said. "I am—"

"I know who you are, Faelin vara'Traejyn. I am Razka. I shared meat and mead with both your father and grandfather before the betrayal at Kyrtigaen Pass."

"My family—"

"I know. I have not come here for vengeance. I bring a warning. As I said, you are being hunted. Once your charge freed Grandfather Shadow, he began tossing around enough divine power for every Adept within a hundred leagues to feel it. You have been gone too long, son of Traejyn, and have forgotten what life holds for the faithful in Kingdom-controlled lands."

Faelin felt the muscles in his face begin to tighten, but he forced them to smooth out. Razka might take any perceived anger or frustration as a challenge, and Faelin chose his battles far more carefully than that. Razka was wrong about one thing: though Faelin had been gone for several years, he would never forget the constant danger to those who worshipped one of the five greater gods in Kingdom lands.

"How much time do I have?" Faelin asked.

"For the Brotherhood of the Night," Razka said, "Half a day at the most. For the House Floraen Inquisitors, a few minutes at best."

Faelin suddenly found it difficult to breathe. "Will you help us?"

"I am helping. Don't ask for more than is offered."

"I meant no offense," Faelin said. "Thank you for what aid you do give. Now excuse me. Julianna and I must put some distance between us and our enemies."

Razka stared Faelin in the eye, looked him up and down, and then nodded.

Faelin turned and raced back to where he had left Julianna.

EIGHT

Carmine could barely hear the sounds of the Brothers breaking camp above the patter of raindrops and wind through the trees. He'd gone a little away from the camp to compose himself before travelling. He hadn't slept well again, having spent the night mourning for Nicco and lusting for an absent Sylvie after rejecting her from his bed again. The hollow pain was still there between his stomach and heart, but not nearly so much since he had decided to fill it with thoughts of finding Julianna and giving her to a Daemyn.

Behind him, footsteps crunched through the leaves and brambles. Whoever it was couldn't be much of a threat if they were moving so clumsily.

"Carmine?" Sylvie said.

Carmine turned. She stood there, wrapped in a cloak, hair matted against her face from the rain. Her blue eyes bore into his with something more than anger.

"You should be about the dishes, your Excellency," Carmine said. "Hardin may have you whipped for shirking your duties."

"Oh, I'm sure there will be no whippings." Sylvie took a step closer to him. "Just as I'm sure I won't be walking, and I won't be sleeping under the wagon anymore."

Sylvie shed her cloak. Aside from her boots, she was naked underneath. Somehow having only those boots on made the sight of her even more arousing. In the full light of day, Carmine lost himself in following the slight curves of her body. A small part of his mind wondered how she had gotten away from the camp and gotten undressed before an alarm was raised, but the rest of him watched dumbly as she came closer and closer. He stiffened a little more with each step she took.

It seemed like it took years for her to travel the distance between them, and when she finally stood before him, she reached for his belt. Her touch reawakened Carmine, and he realized that he was losing control of this. He grabbed at her hands to stop her. She reached up and slapped him, not hard enough to actually hurt him, but enough to stun him for a moment.

"You will not stop me, Marquis D'Mario." Sylvie's voice cracked like a driver's whip. Carmine found himself unable to deny her command any more than a team of horses or oxen could deny the whip that drove them. "There is no Brotherhood here with us. It is just you, a marquis, and me a countess." Her hands undid his belt and loosened his pants while she spoke. "You will obey me. And I command you to stand still."

She pulled his pants around his ankles, and his knees nearly buckled when her mouth became occupied with something other than speaking. He cupped the sides of her head, and maneuvered them a few paces away so that he could lean against a tree. Let her have this illusion that she controlled him while they were alone. He knew where the real power between them lay. Sylvie looked up at him, and the hatred had crept back into her eyes.

Carmine smiled as he leaned back and let her fumble her way through this – now that the initial shock of her brazenness had subsided, it became apparent how awkward this was for her. Yes, he still had the power here. That she hated him so much and still willingly gave herself made it that much sweeter. But she had made her life easier; she would ride the wagon, and she saved herself from the attentions of Hardin's Daemyns.

As he helped guide her through the task of pleasing him, Carmine heard a twig snap. Sylvie had obviously heard it as well, because she attempted to pull her head away from his groin. Carmine moved his right hand to the back of her head to keep her in place and glanced toward where he had heard the sound. Jorgen stood there, watching them. It took the Brother a few moments to realize that he had been noticed. Jorgen's attention had been focused on Sylvie rather than Carmine. When Jorgen's gaze finally drifted upward to meet Carmine's there was no trace of the deference that the Nightbrother usually held when in the presence of an Adept.

"I trust that this is important," Carmine said.

"Yes, Adept."

At the sound of Jorgen's voice, Sylvie tried harder to pull away. Carmine pushed on the back of her head, so much so that she choked a little. She would learn who was the master here.

"The Daemyn hounds have found something," Jorgen said.

"What is it?" Carmine asked.

"You'd best come see," Jorgen replied. "The hounds are in a frenzy."

Carmine released Sylvie's head. "We can continue this in my tent this evening."

Jorgen's lips tightened and he glared at Sylvie. With this look, along with Jorgen's volunteering for the middle watch each night, as well as Sylvie's decline in complaining, Carmine realized that Sylvie must have been granting Jorgen some favors while the rest of the camp was asleep. It made no matter to Carmine. She was his now, and her willingness to please a commoner like Jorgen actually fit perfectly into Carmine's plans for her.

"Take me to the hounds," Carmine said as he pulled up his trousers.

Jorgen spun, and Carmine followed the Brother through the trees.

The Daemyn hounds strained against their tethers, nearly pulling away from the Brothers holding them. In truth, if the hounds had wanted to be free, no human hand could have held them. Only the bargain made between Hardin and the Daemyns who had possessed the hounds kept them under control.

Carmine strode over to the hounds. He scratched one behind the ear. It was strange that the Daemyns seemed to like that while in the dog's body. In their natural form, such a thing would have been demeaning at best.

"What is it, boy?" Carmine asked in a soothing tone. He couldn't call it by name; he didn't know it. Daemyns gave out their names sparingly at best.

"*Zuzak taruzika,*" the hound growled. *I smell miracles.*

"Excellent," Carmine replied. "Where?"

"*Tzaasna, gaz tzaasna.*" *Close, very close.*

The creature led Carmine to a sapling that had been blown apart. Looking about, Carmine saw splinters littering the ground around the tree.

"Can you follow this trail?" Carmine asked.

"*Aztu. Gaz mordu.*" *Yes. Very fresh.*

"It's a good day for us lads," Carmine said. "The hounds have their scent."

All around him, the Brothers cheered.

Carmine turned to Jorgen. "Ride and inform Adept Hardin that we have them. I'm taking a few men and one hound so that we don't lose her. He can follow with the others."

As Jorgen ran off, Carmine had to resist the urge to let the Daemyn hounds loose. Daemyn hounds were not known for their discrimination while hunting. Sending them after Julianna would be far too quick a punishment for her. She wouldn't be much use as breeding stock if one of the creatures devoured her soul.

NINE

"That's what we've been chasing?" Santo asked in a whisper. "A girl barely old enough to call herself an adult by Komati custom?"

The girl in question stood with her back to them, her dark hair hung down to her waist in a dark braid. She wore a man's clothes and had a rapier belted at her side. The rain that trickled down on the two Inquisitors – they had released the miracle for sake of stealth – didn't touch her. Shadows cast by the meager fire next to her stretched out and formed a roof over her. She wore one of the Morigahnti scarves – Luciano believed they were called *Galad'fana* – around her head and shoulders.

"She may be more than what she appears," Luciano replied, also whispering.

"But—" Santo started, but Luciano waved him to silence.

The younger man had received many honors. Few men who joined the Inquisitors rarely came to the order without some sort of decoration. Santo was no different, having bravely headed dangerous missions against heathens in nearly every Kingdom protectorate, but he had never served in Koma. Despite Kingdom propaganda, people other than the Adepts of the Great Houses could draw divine power into the world as miracles, using dedicated foci. Every Inquisitor knew this, but only Inquisitors who had fought against the Morigahnti understood that some of those Morigahnti possessed more power than any Adept.

"I want to get the Faerii blades," Luciano whispered.

Santo's gaze shifted between Luciano and the girl. He jerked his head toward her. Luciano replied by slowly turning his head so that he faced back to the horses. Santo's lips parted in a silent snarl, but after a moment, he sighed quietly, and nodded. Together, they retreated back to their horses. Faerii steel was not usually carried while scouting, because some otherworldly creatures, Daemyns not the least of them, could detect the substance if it came close enough.

They reached the horses, and Santo went about collecting the four egg-sized stones placed in a square around the animals. He picked them up in the proper order, first brown, then green, then gray, then white. If anyone had tried to cross the invisible barrier or remove the stones in any other order, they would receive an almost certainly fatal surprise. Sometimes a horse would try to move beyond that barrier, despite all the training that Inquisitor horses received, and die. It was better to have the occasional dead horse than let the tools of the Inquisition fall into the hands of heathens and the unrighteous.

With the barrier down, they went to the horses. Santo slid his hand between the saddle and saddle blanket and produced a thin, yet long-bladed parrying dagger. Luciano pulled his walking cane out of his bedroll. It was an odd thing to carry on a journey through the Koma wilderness, but it concealed a rapier-like blade of Faerii steel.

They looked at each other, nodded, and turned back toward where they'd left the Morigahnti girl.

The girl was there, not ten paces away. She leaned against a tree and stared at them with hard, storm-cloud-gray eyes. She might have been beautiful if not for the fresh scar that cut down the right side of her face. Her right hand held a rapier casually at her side, and her left hand flipped a dagger end over end – a dagger with a blade of Faerii steel. The girl gave him a flirtatious wink. That scar held his attention the most, especially because it was on the right side of her face. Luciano's breath caught in his throat, and his innards churned as if he were once more a twittering disciple at the Academy of the Sun.

"Good morning, High Blood Adept Inquisitors," she said. "How may I serve the Kingdom?"

"Whom do I have the honor of addressing?" Santo asked.

Santo had obviously not studied Komati lore. Why should he have? Luciano had been no different when he had first come here six years ago. He thought that this would be just like any other protectorate. Hard lessons with scars to prove it had taught him otherwise, and he had studied the history and mythology of this land with almost the same fervor that he followed the teachings of All Father Sun. No Komati would mar their face in such a way unless they were mad and wished to be killed or they were…

"I am the Lord Morigahn," the girl replied.

Santo laughed. "Well, Lord Morigahn, if you come peaceably, we may allow you to die with your soul intact."

Luciano cringed.

The girl returned her rapier to its sheath.

"Try to take me, Inquisitor," she said, as she cleaned her fingernails with the dagger, "and my god will eat your soul."

TEN

"Julianna," Faelin said as he burst out of the brush. "We have to—"

Faelin slid to a stop on the wet pine needles. She was gone. He scanned the ground and saw a pair of footprints leading away from the camp. After about thirty or forty paces, Julianna's tracks joined with another pair of footprints.

"Shades!" Faelin swore. "What has she done?"

"*Tuska*!" Julianna yelled up ahead. This was followed by the sound of splintering wood and screaming horses.

"*Seguindus midian aparthan*!" a distinctly male voice boomed. It sounded like the holy tongue of All Father Sun. Light flashed and the sound of flames roared.

Faelin broke into a sprint. Leaves and branches whipped at his face, and underbrush threatened to trip him up as he rushed headlong toward this erupting battle of miracles.

"*Galad mina varjela*." Julianna's voice croaked the miracle, a miracle that was too strong for her to attempt. She was channeling too much divine energy too quickly and wouldn't last much longer. Faelin was amazed that she could still stand.

Faelin only heard her because he had gotten close enough to make out the figures through the trees. Dozens of shadows stretched toward Julianna, dancing and weaving around her, creating a cylinder that protected her from a man wearing the golden breast plate and scarlet cape of a House Floraen Inquisitor. The Inquisitor struck at the hardened shadows with a rapier and dagger, but could not pierce them.

A second Inquisitor, this one a few years older than the other, walked toward Julianna with a globe of blazing light held in a hand above his head. The closer he got, the more the shadows protecting Julianna faded.

Faelin raised the crossbow, hands clenching the weapon as he thought, *Which one? Which one*? He took aim.

Before he loosed the quarrel, he heard something crashing through the brush off to his right. Faelin turned and saw a handful of men in black leather armor, faces concealed by bone-white skull masks, rushing toward them. Beyond them, a man wearing the mantle of an Adept of Old Uncle Night sat on a horse. Beside him, a huge, hairless dog with luminescent eyes strained on a leather leash.

So much for half a day.

Faelin aimed again, this time at the Night Adept. The Night Adept seemed to notice Faelin's attention and turned to meet his gaze. Now that Faelin had a good view of the Adept's face, he recognized Carmine D'Mario. One side of Carmine's face curved into an amused smirk. At the same time Faelin released the crossbow bolt, Carmine let go of the leash which held the Daemyn hound.

ELEVEN

As soon as he let go of the Daemyn hound, Carmine pitched himself off his horse. Faelin vara'Traejyn had always been more clever than he had any right to be. Carmine didn't want to gamble whether Faelin knew that he could banish the Daemyn within the hound by killing the man who had summoned it. While Hardin had summoned this one, Faelin wouldn't know that. As Carmine toppled from the horse, he heard more than felt something pass within a hand's span of his head. Faelin might be clever, but not clever enough by a few heartbeats, and now the Daemyn hound would ensure that he would never be that clever again.

Carmine hit the ground with a muddy splash. His horse had not been fully trained for combat, and it bolted the moment Carmine fell. Carmine watched his horse run for a total of three heartbeats, then he scampered behind a tree. The Daemyn hound had almost reached Faelin, and Julianna was fighting the two Inquisitors. Carmine could easily support the Nightbrothers and the Daemyn hound from this tactical position rather than put himself in more danger than he needed to.

TWELVE

When Luciano got within ten paces of the Lord Morigahn, the divine light he carried pierced the shadows protecting her enough for Santo's blades to actually penetrate the defense. It wasn't enough for him to make a clean strike, though. The shadows still slowed him so that it appeared that he was practicing his swordplay at half normal speed in order to focus on proper form. The Lord Morigahn easily dodged him, but it forced her to stop speaking miracles – at least for the moment.

Luciano took another step forward. He could tell that she was exhausted. Her gaunt cheeks told him that she shouldn't even be able to stand, much less continue fighting. Another step forward and he saw the crazed feral look her eyes held. Even as she spun away from Santo, those steel eyes met his then glanced over his shoulder.

"Get down," she snarled just as Luciano heard the sound of someone running up behind.

After a moment's calculation and silent prayer to All Father Sun, Luciano dropped.

"*Mina kehia turvata*!" Julianna spoke, and she pushed her hand outward.

A burst of wind flew past Luciano pulling at his clothes and hair. Had he been standing, he had no doubt it would have taken him off his feet or worse. Glancing over his shoulder, he saw a group of Nightbrothers picked up off their feet and flung through the trees as easily as the leaves and twigs the wind carried in its wake. The Lord Morigahn's miracle had only eliminated about half of the Nightbrothers. Six more ran toward them, curved short swords drawn. To his right, a Daemyn hound barreled down on a man who was hurriedly loading a crossbow. This other man was obviously not with the Brotherhood, but had he come as an ally to the Lord Morigahn or had he stumbled into this as an unlucky happenstance?

Luciano had a choice to make. Did he help Santo against the Lord Morigahn, or did he try and work with her to fight the Brotherhood? That was the sanest option. Could he even convince her that their only hope was to work together?

Luciano threw his orb of light at a spot between the man with the crossbow and the Daemyn hound.

He drew on the dominions of Light and Day, and called, "*Lacceo.*"

The orb of light exploded.

THIRTEEN

Julianna screamed as the Inquisitor's blade bit into her left arm just below the shoulder.

Thank you Sister Wind for protecting my sword arm.

The silent prayer came into Julianna's mind by pure habit. Even as she thought the words, she clenched her teeth. A great eruption of pain blinded her as the experience of the knife cutting her face returned in all its agony. The Lord Morigahn could pray to no other gods besides Grandfather Shadow. Breaking every habit that her Koma heritage had instilled in her would be bothersome at best.

Even through the searing pain, Julianna heard someone chuckle above her. "Goodbye, Lord Morigahn." Whoever it was spoke her name with an edge of disdainful sarcasm.

"No, Santo," someone else yelled. "We need her."

Julianna didn't wait to find out whether or not the protest was heeded. She rolled to her left, soaking her clothes on the muddy turf as she scrambled to her hands and knees, and scurried away from the Inquisitors and Nightbrothers as fast as she could – at least she hoped it was away; she couldn't be sure in her blindness and pain. She stopped short when her head collided with something hard. Flashing lights danced in her vision.

FOURTEEN

Faelin saw the orb of light land in a puddle. The water boiled and sizzled from the heat. He'd seen this enough in the battlefields of Heidenmarch and turned around before the Inquisitor called out his miracle. Light blazed all around Faelin, warming him for a moment as he fled the Daemyn hound and headed to where Julianna had run headlong into a tree.

One of the Inquisitors – the younger one – stalked toward Julianna, sword raised to strike.

Faelin sprinted toward them and flung the crossbow as hard as he could. It caught the Inquisitor in the shoulder. He reeled from the blow, and better yet, dropped his sword.

Faelin was on him by the time he recovered. He grabbed a handful of the Inquisitor's cloak with his left hand and a handful of hair in his right. The Inquisitor tried to pull away, but Faelin slammed his knee into the Inquisitor's hip. The Inquisitor gave a grunt of pain as his leg gave out. Faelin let go of the man's hair and brought his elbow down on the soft spot between his skull and neck. The Inquisitor crumpled.

Faelin heard splashing on the ground to his right, and his scalp prickled. He'd learned to heed that sensation ever since the battlefield in Heidenmarch. The one time he hadn't, a pike had pierced his left thigh.

Dropping to his left, Faelin rolled toward Julianna. Something sharp cut into his right shoulder. He grimaced at the pain. He reached out and grabbed hold of what had stabbed, hoping – praying – that it was the Inquisitor's sword. Faelin could never hope to fight the Nightbrothers with just a dirk. His fingers closed around it. It was flat, thin, and sharp. He grasped it with just enough pressure so that it wouldn't slice his palm and fingers to ribbons. He came to his feet, holding a parrying dagger by the blade, barely a hand's length from the hilt.

Its blade had been forged of Faerii steel, but Faelin had no time to marvel over this.

One of the Nightbrothers rushed Faelin, giving him no time to adjust his grip. The Nightbrother lunged. Faelin brought up his left elbow and spun. He avoiding the attack and connected with the Nightbrother's skull helmet. Faelin hadn't intended the blow to hurt, just knock the helm askew in order to distract his enemy for a moment. Faelin completed the spin, using his momentum to help him pierce the leather armor. The knife slid easily into the Nightbrother's neck. Faelin's hand slid up the blade. It felt like fire burned his arm all the way to the shoulder as the blade cut through skin and muscle of his hand and bit into bone.

Ignoring the pain as best he could, Faelin scanned the area as the corpse slid off the blade. A Nightbrother stalked toward Faelin. His eyes flicked from the body of his fallen comrade to Faelin. He seemed less than eager to rush into a fight with someone willing to cripple his hand to defeat a foe. Faelin used that time to shift his newly-acquired sword into his left hand. Another Nightbrother was on his knees next to the Inquisitor Faelin had incapacitated. Blood flowed from a fresh wound on the Inquisitor's neck. All the other Nightbrothers were charging the second Inquisitor.

"No, you fools!" Carmine's voice screamed in the distance. "Let the hound have that one. Get the girl! Get the girl!"

The Nightbrother who had killed the younger Inquisitor stood and joined the one already facing Faelin. Faelin raised his sword. His other arm burned as if he'd thrust it into a blacksmith's fire.

Perhaps he could hold them long enough for Julianna to come to her senses and escape.

FIFTEEN

Luciano wanted to scream.

Why couldn't Santo have listened? The Nightbrothers had done what they always did: they struck while potential allies fought. Luciano could do nothing for Santo now, and the younger Inquisitor's Faerii blade was lost for the moment. If Luciano died here, either the Brotherhood or the Morigahnti would gain The Detector and his Faerii blade. The Inquisition would be unlikely to regain them.

As the Daemyn hound rushed toward him, Luciano grabbed the nine-pointed star pendant that hung from his neck. He could feel All Father Sun's three dominions – Day, Light, and Truth – swirling within it. He closed his eyes and drew on the dominion of Day much more than he'd drawn on any dominion in his life. He didn't know if the miracle would work, but he had to try.

"*Mishrak Amhyr'Shoul, aevidho som vaso mirso aetirumes.*" As the miracle left his lips, exhaustion crushed down on Luciano with such force that he collapsed under its weight.

SIXTEEN

Faelin shifted his left foot, preparing to lunge at the closest Nightbrother. Two more came running up behind the original pair that faced him now. Gods and goddesses, he wished he could read their faces. That would have helped so much in calculating his strategy.

"*Tuska,*" Julianna's voice said from behind Faelin.

A bolt of dark energy flew past his ear. For a moment, Faelin thought he could almost hear a voice whispering *kostota* and *Galad*, the words for vengeance and shadow, the two dominions required for that particular miracle. The bolt hit the front Nightbrother in the helmet. The leather skull mask ripped away from the Brother's head, pulling chunks of bone and flesh, as if some invisible hand was pealing a juicy red fruit.

Julianna stepped into line with Faelin. She raised her rapier straight out from her shoulder, tip pointed directly toward one of the Nightbrother's eyes. She stood on her toes, the perfect position of the second aggressive posture of the House Andres academy of defense.

This gave the Brothers a few moments of pause.

"Are you hurt?" Faelin asked.

"A bit." She smiled. "More my pride than anything else."

Julianna placed her free hand on Faelin's shoulder, and she grabbed a handful of his coat.

"Hold on," Julianna said, and the world shifted around them.

SEVENTEEN

"No!" Carmine screamed when he saw Julianna and Faelin vanish.

Carmine stood and came out from his hiding place. The Night-brothers were regrouping; well, those that were still living or capable of moving.

Out of the corner of his eye, Carmine saw something moving through the trees. His head snapped around. Was that a pair of wolves stalking through the gloom of the mist? That couldn't be anything but bad.

"Orders, Adept Carmine?" one of the Brothers asked.

Carmine barely heard him. His gaze swept through the trees. Wolf sightings were rare, though not unheard of in Koma, and the fighting should have driven any nearby wolves away. But still, wolves did not concern Carmine; the Nightbrothers and the Daemyn hound could handle wolves. A quiet fear whispered throughout the Brotherhood of the Night that not all the Stormseekers had died at the Battle of Kyrtigaen Pass. There were some, the First Adept included, who believed that someday those shape-shifting wolves would return seeking revenge. This would be a very awkward time for the Stormseekers to begin aiding the Morigahnti again – very awkward for him and the remaining seven Brothers.

"I see seven of you still capable of fighting," Carmine said. "I leave it to you gentlemen to fix it so we have a more favorable number."

It didn't take long. The six healthiest turned on the weakest Brother. As they struggled, Carmine considered the possibility that Stormseekers would involve themselves now, *if* he had actually seen them. The Brotherhood had killed two Lords Morigahn since Kyrtigaen Pass, and the Seekers had not interfered.

"Orders now, Adept?" one of the Brothers asked when there were only six of them standing.

"We will return to Adept Hardin," Carmine said. "Julianna has eluded us for now."

He whistled. The Daemyn hound returned. It had been sniffing about the place where the Inquisitor had vanished. Carmine had not been able to hear the Inquisitor's miracle, so he had no idea where that man had vanished to.

Carmine knelt down next to the hound and scratched it behind the ear.

"Find the Lord Morigahn," Carmine said. "Do not harm her, but kill the man with her. Harry the girl until she drops. Give her no time to eat or rest, but do not touch her. I have plans for that one. Kill anything that gets between you and her. Do you understand?"

"*Aztu.*" The hound snorted and dashed off into the trees.

If there were any Stormseekers helping Julianna, the Daemyn hound would likely take their attention away from Carmine and his small band of Nightbrothers. As he turned to go after his horse, an idea formed in Carmine's mind.

"You two," he waved at two Brothers at random, "fetch the Inquisitor's corpse."

They did.

"What of the Inquisitors' horses?" one of the Brothers asked.

Carmine couldn't help but smile. "If you can manage to get in a sad-le and stay there, you are welcome to it."

Inquisitors' horses were notoriously difficult to ride for any who were not trained as an Inquisitor, not to mention the little surprises the Inquisitors left behind. To Carmine's knowledge, that was one of the few secrets that the Brotherhood had not learned about the followers of the other gods.

Carmine found his horse a little ways off. Its head snapped up and ears flicked back and forth as he approached, but the animal did not spook. When he got back into the saddle, he rode toward Hardin and the camp. After the Daemyn hound devoured Faelin's soul, taking Julianna would be so much easier. Then, Her Grace, the Duchess Taraen, would begin to learn the true nature of suffering.

EIGHTEEN

The sensation of being pulled in every direction at once faded, and Faelin fell to his knees. Bile rose in his stomach, and he succeeded in choking most of it down. He spat out the bit of it that managed to come up and got to his feet.

Two Saifreni horses stood black and regal in a clearing not even twenty paces from them. The saddles on them were the high-backed style favored by House Floraen, and even from this distance, Faelin could see the fine craftsmanship that had gone into the tooling of great yellow and red suns all over the saddles.

He turned to Julianna.

She leaned against a tree. Dark, half-moon circles sagged under her eyes.

"We have to go," she said. "They'll be here any minute."

"Who will be?" Faelin asked.

"The Inquisitors."

She pushed off the tree she had been leaning against and stumbled. Faelin grabbed her arm. Her sleeve rubbed against the cuts on his hand, but Faelin pushed the pain aside. He could deal with his injury once they returned to the horses and got underway. He took a step and then realized he had no idea where the animals might be.

"Which way are the horses?" Faelin asked.

Julianna waved in the direction she was facing.

Faelin half-supported, half-dragged Julianna as they raced through the trees. Already his blood soaked into the sleeve of her chemise around his hand.

"Don't go so fast," Julianna said, "or we'll get there too soon."

"Too soon? We can't get there soon enough for my mind."

To emphasize this, Faelin began to move faster.

"No." Julianna grabbed a sapling and pulled herself to a stop, and subsequently out of Faelin's grip.

That sent bolts of pain shooting from his palm up to his shoulder.

Faelin turned toward Julianna, ready with a rebuke, but she continued. "If we keep going at that pace, we'll meet at least one of ourselves back by the horses." She paused for breath. "And be quiet, or we'll hear ourselves."

"What did you do to us?" Faelin dropped his tone.

She leaned on the sapling and took a deep breath. "I took us back before the fight started. We should get back to the camp a few moments after I left, which will give us plenty of time to get a head start on getting away from our enemies. Now give me a hand and don't move too fast. I just need a few moments of rest after all that I've just done."

Faelin offered his hand. Julianna took it. He led her toward the camp in as quick a pace as she could handle without stumbling. He remained silent as they moved through the woods.

They walked in silence, but after a few moments, Faelin couldn't contain himself.

"What were you thinking?" he asked.

"I needed," the words came out between her ragged breaths, as if speaking them took all her concentration, "to practice."

"Practice? This was a battle, not practice."

"Let them come. The Brotherhood. The Inquisitors. Let them all come." Julianna's eyes grew wide and her lips curved upward in an eager smile.

"They did come. Both of them. And they almost killed us. Be thankful the Inquisitors didn't have any Draqons with them, or we would be dead."

"*Aen Morigahnti te kis ulos taetso. Yn'mina Morigahn'uljas. Mina te kis ulos. Mina viholenti raesu ansa mina varjosta yskin.*"

Faelin suppressed the urge to scream. Julianna spoke the same words that Saent Kaethan spoke just before the Battle of Ykthae Wood. *The Morigahnti do not flee from battle. I am the Lord Morigahn. I do not run. My enemies will fall by my faith alone.* That short speech had inspired the few hundred Morigahnti present to fight with such ferocity that, although only forty-nine of those Morigahnti had lived, thousands of their enemies fell for each Morigahnti slain.

That outburst had given Faelin much to consider. From what he knew of Julianna, she should not know much about the Morigahnti – or should she? How much had changed in Koma in the last five years? Had her uncle's family joined the Morigahnti? Khellan had been marked as the Lord Morigahn also. Had Julianna known this? Had she received more from Grandfather Shadow than just the ability to speak *Galad'laman*? Had he also given her at least some portion of the previous Lords Morigahn's memories?

He heard twigs and branches snapping to his left. Faelin watched himself rushing to find Julianna. It was a strange sight, and Faelin couldn't tell if the sudden dizziness he felt was a creation of his own mind, some lingering effect of Julianna's ability, or loss of blood still oozing from his injured hand. Would it get worse if he got closer? He decided he didn't want to know.

"Now," Julianna said, "we can return to the horses."

Faelin decided not to continue their argument. Julianna was still too traumatized by her experiences to listen to any rational discourse. Now was not the time to convince her of the folly of her choices, but rather, they needed to put as much distance between them and the disaster behind.

They returned to where they had left the horses. Vendyr and the other steeds chewed happily on the brush where Faelin had tied them. He silently thanked Grandfather Shadow that he had not planned to camp here for the evening and so the horses were still saddled.

Faelin slid his newly acquired Faerii blade into his belt and helped Julianna into Vendyr's saddle. Then he went to the spare horses and let them go in different directions.

"It may not be much of a distraction," Faelin said. "But it's better than not trying anything at all. It may even throw them off our trail for a bit."

As Faelin stepped into his stirrup, his horse's head jerked straight up. Its ears flattened against its head, and its eyes went wide. Faelin barely flung himself away before the horse bolted into the trees. Had he acted even a heartbeat later, he would likely have been trapped in the stirrup, and the horse would be dragging him for only the gods knew how long.

He didn't have any time to consider this, or what to do about his lack of a horse, when something large and solid slammed into him. Faelin turned as he fell. Hot breath blasted him in the face. It smelled of death and sickness. A great weight pressed down upon him. Faelin struggled to escape, but he only managed to get his left forearm up in time to keep the Daemyn hound from closing its jaws around his throat. His stomach threatened to expel its contents, but Faelin tightened every muscle inside him to keep it under control. He heard himself screaming while at the same time he determined that dying from the infection of the creature's bite was better than having his soul devoured. With his free hand – the hand that had been sliced nearly to ribbons by the Faerii blade – Faelin punched the Daemyn hound repeatedly in the head. It didn't seem to notice, and it didn't try to pull its jaws away from Faelin's arm. It seemed more content to try and chew its way through the bone. It might also succeed, unless Faelin could figure out a way get the creature off him long enough to get the Faerii blade out of his belt.

NINETEEN

Vendyr spun in circles, eyes rolled back and almost completely white with fear. He had tried to bolt, but thankfully, he'd been facing the Daemyn hound when it appeared. The horse had to wheel or else flee directly toward the attacking predator. Exactly as Julianna predicted, Vendyr turned to the left. He'd always been inclined to that direction. Rather than fight to straighten him, Julianna kept a steady pressure on his reins, keeping Vendyr spinning to the left. He fought her, but she kept his neck bent so much that his nose nearly touched his left flank.

As she kept leading Vendyr in those tight circles, Julianna held both reins in her left hand and drew her mother's knife with the right. Mother's words came back from across fourteen years, *Take this, Julianna; it will protect you against anything less than a god.*

After two more turns, Vendyr began to settle. Julianna allowed him to straighten just as they were coming to face away from the Daemyn hound. She leaned forward, tapped both knees into Vendyr's flanks, and held on with every bit of strength she had left. Just as she had trained him, Vendyr kicked out with his hind legs. It was a trick she'd taught him to amuse herself at the expense of overly arrogant lords who attempted to become too familiar with her on long hunting trips.

It felt like both of Vendyr's back hooves connected with the hound. It yipped and whined like a real dog. Julianna turned Vendyr to face the thing.

The hound had already recovered. It was stalking toward Faelin, who had pointed a parrying dagger of the same kind of metal as Mother's dagger at the Daemyn. Faelin was coated in blood, and his left arm looked as if it would need months to heal. Blood also dripped from the hand that held the weapon.

Julianna screamed, "Once we were like wolves!" and kicked Vendyr into a charge.

The hound's gaze, eerie orbs that glowed like a dying ember in a fire, darted between Julianna and Faelin.

In that moment of hesitation, Faelin struck. He lunged more quickly than Julianna would have believed possible had she not seen it. Uncle Alyx had purchased the services of a Floraen Maestro of D'fence for Marcus' twenty-first birthday gift. Even that man who had dedicated his life to the study of refining the science of sword play could not move as fast as Faelin. His speed bordered on Julianna's talent for shifting time and space.

Faelin buried the parrying dagger in the hound's neck up to the hilt. The Daemyn snapped at him, but Faelin leapt to the side, drawing his blade out, creating a gash as long as Julianna's forearm on the creature's flank.

This distracted it long enough for Julianna to strike. She would have never succeeded if it had been a normal-sized dog; it would have been too short. But the Daemyn hound was just large enough for Julianna to stab it in the back of the neck as she rode past. She twisted her knife as she withdrew it from the monster's flesh, creating a gaping hole that spurted brackish, green-gray blood.

The Daemyn hound roared. The sound was like nothing that ever came from a natural animal. It was like a wolf trying to howl with all the ice of winter caught in its throat. Though the sound was cold, it brought back the heat of the sickness that had afflicted Julianna when she had been fourteen.

The hound lunged for Faelin, but its injured leg would not support it. It collapsed. Faelin darted in, giving it another two slashes. This game went on for a few minutes. As the creature slowed, Faelin cut it more and more. Plants died where its blood spilled to the ground.

At last, the creature gave one final howl and collapsed in on itself, becoming an empty husk.

"They will have heard that," Faelin said as he came over to her; Vendyr would not approach the Daemyn hound's corpse. "We must go."

Julianna sheathed her knife, reached down, and helped Faelin onto Vendyr behind her.

"Which direction?" she asked.

"Southeast," Faelin said, pointing

They had been going west since he found her, but Julianna didn't feel like arguing. She was so tired she couldn't think straight. She prayed – to Grandfather Shadow this time – that they found someplace to tend Faelin's wounds before too long, or Julianna was going to be facing the rest of her journey as the Lord Morigahn alone.

TWENTY

Inquisitor Luciano blinked awake. All Father Sun shone into his eyes, blinding him. Luciano groaned as he covered his eyes with his forearm and rolled onto his back. He lay on something damp and spongy. Had he been asleep or unconscious? His head ached and his stomach churned as if he were wine sick. He sat up, pushed his palms into his eyes, and laced his fingers into the hair that hung down past his forehead. Santo was dead, and his Faerii-steel blade was in the hands of the Morigahnti, or at least had been; perhaps the Brotherhood of the Night had claimed possession. Luciano wondered about the Morigahnti. Had they survived the fight as well? He had no doubt that this woman who claimed to be the Lord Morigahn was capable of dealing with a handful of Nightbrothers, even those led by an Adept of Night with them. The question was whether or not she could deal with a Daemyn hound as well.

Luciano got to his feet and took in his surroundings. Bodies of Nightbrothers lay around him, naked now. The Brotherhood cared not for burial rituals. For them, death was the ritual. Flies buzzed in the area, but he saw no maggots eating away at the exposed flesh of their injuries. Santo's body was gone, which troubled Luciano a great deal. Would the Brotherhood of the Night be able to discern secrets from the corpse of an Inquisitor? Such a notion was preposterous. For that, they would need the body's soul, and All Father Sun took the soul of a fallen Inquisitor into His paradise immediately upon death and rewarded the loyal follower by removing him or her from the Cycle of Life, Death, and Rebirth.

Luciano left the scene and made his way back to where he and Santo had first seen the Lord Morigahn. When he arrived, he found the corpse of a Daemyn hound crisscrossed with cuts and punctures. The man who had come to the Lord Morigahn's aid must still have Santo's Faerii-steel blade, though Luciano suspected it was likely that the Lord Morigahn had claimed the weapon for herself.

Luciano brought The Detector out of his pocket. He twisted two of the five knobs at the top. Both hands swiveled to the southeast. Luciano started walking back toward the horses. It would take time to unsaddle, groom, and feed both his horse, Emperor and Santo's horse, Dawn Chaser, but having both of them would cut down on the time between now and when he could reclaim the Faerii-steel blade and bring this Lord Morigahn before the Sun King's justice.

CHOICES

If we mortals are so far beneath the gods, why do they constantly interfere in our affairs?
– Kavala

Kostota na aen paras kostota.
"Revenge is the best revenge"
The First Law of Grandfather Shadow

ONE

In the fading light of dusk, two figures ascended the slopes of Mount Kolmonen. One, dressed in silks of pearl-white and sky-blue that did little to cover her shapely form, floated alongside the other who climbed a narrow trail. The climber wore heavy furs and wools to fight the cold and biting wind. It had taken him two days to reach this high. The floating figure would have saved him the trouble, if he had only asked. But he preferred to make the journey himself and would not accept help from any Eldar.

Human behavior puzzled Kahddria.

The goddess of wind had possessed many other names over the course of human existence, many of those names forgotten, which brought no small amount of sorrow to her heart. She missed some of the more poetic things humans had called her, as well as the grand stories those lost cultures used to tell about her. Now she was known to most in the current human era merely as the lesser goddess, Sister Wind, and most of the stories had grown bland.

"Why do you think that most mortals have simplified the Eldar?" Kahddria asked. "Once there were great mythologies created around us. Now we've become nothing more than a collection of simple stories and superstitions, not counting the Kingdom High Blood. Why do you think that is?"

The human climbing the thin trail below her stopped and looked up at her.

"You have my complete respect, Kahddria," he shouted up into the wind. His voice possessed none of the respect he claimed. "But if we're actually going to converse, would you please come down so that I don't have to crane my neck."

"Of course." Kahddria floated down next to him. "Now, Maxian, give me your suspicions."

"You answered your own question," the man said. "For the last thousand years the Kingdom has conquered and subjugated most of the other lands on this continent. As they stamped out the worship of the Greater Eldar, they also diminished human interest in the Lesser Eldar as well. With their Draqon armies, it's easy for the common man to think that the Kingdom is destined to rule the world. I'd be bitter against the gods if I believed that simplified view of the universe."

"What an intriguing idea," Kahddria said. "Would you share this idea with the others?"

"I don't have to," Maxian replied, and continued his climb. "I've discussed these thoughts with several of the Eldar. Some agree with me, some disagree. I don't really care what any of you believe."

She mulled this over for a moment and opened her mouth to tell him that it did matter, but that wouldn't do any good. Maxian's mind was made up, at least as far as the Eldar were concerned. He wouldn't change his mind about them any more than he would accept her help, no matter how innocently the offer was made. Maxian was one of those rare individuals who had cried out against the Eldar, begging freedom from their intervention in his life, for good or for ill. Due to the Ykthae Accord, any mortal that asked for autonomy from celestial influence would be granted that wish. After that, the mortal couldn't be freed from the influence of just one part of the celestial realms; the mortal had to separate himself from *all* aspects of the realms beyond the physical. However, though Maxian had done just that, it hadn't stopped him from involving himself in celestial politics, which infuriated most of the others because they couldn't do anything to stop him.

"Waiting for you to finish this climb is getting rather tiresome," Kahddria said.

"I never asked you to accompany me. And I never promised to be entertaining."

"Indeed, but you don't have to go out of your way to be so immensely boring."

Maxian shrugged, and continued up the path.

Kahddria left him to his cynicism and flew to a cave near the summit. It grew colder as she approached the cave, colder even than the elevation should dictate. The temperature didn't bother her; she summoned a breeze of warm air from the tip of the southern-most island of Inis O'lean. There were dozens of different kinds of wildflowers growing along that coastline. The scents of those flowers mixed with the salty sea air to create the sweetest aroma of the whole world. She set that wind spinning around her body and separated it from the winds that howled at the summit of Mount Kolmonen.

When she entered the cave, Kahddria saw she wasn't the last to arrive – even taking Maxian into consideration. Two of her fellow Lesser Eldar sat around a table made of skulls. In the normally dark eyes of those skulls, Kahddria thought she saw the hint of eyes pleading for rest. These were souls from the Realm of the Godless Dead. Yrgaeshkil sat in a chair of miscellaneous bones and rotting flesh. She wore a more subdued form at the moment. Her only Daemynic features were the two leathery wings sprouting from her shoulders. Other than that, she looked like a young woman not even thirty years old, dark and beautiful.

Yrgaeshkil possessed power over the dominion of Lies, which she allowed some of her husband's followers to use. She had also enjoyed a great deal of freedom in the thousand years since the Lords of Order had imprisoned her husband. A few days ago, this blatant use of her husband's domain would likely have drawn the King of Order's attentions, but so much had changed since then. It was still a risk, because none of them knew how far they could push the boundaries of the Ykthae Accord.

Next to her was Skaethak, or Sister Winter, as mortals called her. This evening she was an albino waif of a girl, lounging on a couch of snow and ice.

"Is Innaya coming?" Kahddria asked as she floated over to the table.

"I believe so." Skaethak's voice came out as a whispered tinkle, and bits of frost formed in the air with her words.

"I am indeed here," replied a husky voice.

A searing light pierced the cave's gloom, and a tall, voluptuous woman stood at the last vacant spot at the table. Innaya, the Lady of Dawn, All Father Sun's daughter, even went so far as to wear a human head with blond hair and blue eyes and to dress in glowing plate armor from a culture decimated by the Kingdom centuries before.

"Are you ever going to change your appearance?" Skaethak asked. "It's been over three hundred years since those people were killed."

"One of them was my daughter," Innaya said. "I still mourn her."

"I've told you before," Yrgaeshkil words dripped like poison honey, "you may visit her any time you like."

A sword of light appeared in Innaya's hand. "And be powerless in your *husband's* realm? Hardly."

Yrgaeshkil's face tightened with Innaya's slight inflection on the word husband. The Aengyl smiled sweetly, which caused the Daemyn's features to shift into a more bat-like appearance.

Kahddria had to get control of this gathering or they would likely shorten the summit with their squabbling. She didn't really care about the mountain, but devastation of that level would attract attention. There were some of the Eldar that Kahddria didn't want snooping around in this matter.

"Ladies," Kahddria floated between them, "we're not here to bicker. We're here to discuss matters of great importance."

"Let me make a supposition." Skaethak's whispered voice dripped with sarcasm. "One of *them* is free."

"Yes." Kahddria kept her voice even, though she wanted to pull a hot wind from the Lands of Endless Summer to warm the cold bitch. "I'm surprised you didn't feel it, since it was Galad'Ysoysa who was freed."

"Impossible," Skaethak said. "I would know."

"Why is that?" Yrgaeshkil asked. "He is the God of Secrets; perhaps he is keeping this a secret from you. Lords and Princes! Think a bit. If you were suddenly free from a prison after ten centuries, wouldn't you wait and see what the Lesser are up to, not to mention the state of the mortal world?"

"But what proof do we have?" Innaya asked. "Other than her word, of course?"

"I, too, have sensed his presence through my husband's worshipers."

Innaya snorted out a contemptuous laugh. "I know you'll forgive me if I doubt the one of us at this meeting who bears the title, Mother of Lies."

"Calm down, Innaya," Skaethak said. "I agree with you. What other proof do you have, Kahddria?"

Both Innaya and Skaethak fixed Kahddria with demanding stares. She sighed. She'd forgotten how cynical and suspicious the other Eldar were. Like the other elemental Eldar, Kahddria was more straightforward and less prone to deception than the others, especially the seasons.

"Me," came a voice from the cave's entrance.

All four Lesser Eldar turned. Maxian stood in the cave's mouth. How had he gotten here so fast? He should have been at least another hour away.

"And why should you know that he has returned when Skaethak does not?" Yrgaeshkil asked. "Considering you have removed yourself from celestial influence, why should we believe or trust you?"

Maxian's mouth curved into a smirk which accentuated the scar that ran down the right side of his face. That old wound seemed to darken. His cold eyes did not reflect the smile.

"I have my sources," Maxian said, "sources that no Eldar can touch."

"And who would be more reliable than one of the Lesser Eldar sworn to Galad'Ysoysa?" Skaethak asked.

Kahddria suppressed a smile. She knew Maxian's secret. Few of the other Eldar did; they could not watch him from afar. Kahddria had taken it upon herself to maintain a close watch on the small handful of people who had done as Maxian. She had cultivated relationships with them, which had taken some doing in certain cases. One never knew when it would be advantageous to know someone completely immune to the powers of the Eldar. Thus far, only one member of that small group of mortals on this continent remained aloof of her advances.

"The Stormseekers," Maxian replied.

"Why would they tell you?" Skaethak demanded. "They haven't been involved in the game since…"

"My wife died," Maxian finished. "A few days ago, Razka informed me that Grandfather Shadow had returned and had marked a new Lord Morigahn with his own hand."

Kahddria watched as the other three considered this. They looked back and forth at each other, then at her, trying to gauge what their next course of action should be.

Yrgaeshkil spoke first. "Who is the lucky man that Galad'Ysoysa has chosen?"

"He didn't choose a man," Maxian replied. "He chose a woman. The Stormseekers didn't give me a name, and I don't care."

"If you don't care," Skaethak said, "why are you telling us this?"

Maxian shrugged.

"There are others who know," Kahddria said. "The First Adept of Old Uncle Night, the Speaker of Lies, this new Lord Morigahn, any Morigahnti bonded to a Stormcrow, and any Morigahnti who will hold still long enough for a Morigahnti bonded to a Stormcrow to tell him that Grandfather Shadow has returned."

"There is one other who might know," Maxian said.

"Who is that?" Innaya said, joining the conversation at last.

"The only other man to shed the mantle of the Lord Morigahn without dying," Maxian replied.

"Why should we care about him knowing?" Yrgaeshkil asked.

"Because," Kahddria replied, "he is currently mentoring the Speaker of Lies, giving him access to the First Adept of Old Uncle Night."

Yrgaeshkil's eyes grew wide. As Kahddria suspected, Yrgaeshkil didn't revel in the thought of her husband gaining his freedom. If Kavala felt enough fear from Galad'Ysoysa's return, he might try to free another of the Greater Eldar.

"Think of what that will mean," Maxian said, "if Old Uncle Night and Grandfather Shadow are the only Greater Eldar free in the world."

"He's right," Skaethak said. "We will have to do something. But what?"

"We will have to bring others into this," Innaya said. "Even if we four worked together, we would be sore pressed to defeat one of the Greater Eldar."

"True," Kahddria said. "Then, let us return in one week's time. Bring at least one of your fellows with you. Eight of us might be enough."

"Wait," Innaya said. "What if one of us thinks to curry favor with Galad'Ysoysa by betraying the others?"

"That would be very foolish indeed," Skaethak said. "The very fact that we are at this meeting and having this discussion might be enough for him to punish us, regardless of whether or not we betray the others. We have just plotted to destroy one of the Greater, something that hasn't been done since the First War. None of them will take kindly to that. It's in our best interest to see this through now."

"Agreed," the other three said.

Without another word Skaethak, Yrgaeshkil, and Innaya vanished.

"That went much better than I hoped," Kahddria said. "There is a fight coming. You would prove a very powerful ally."

"I am done fighting. I will bring you information, and as much as I complain, I do enjoy your company at times. However, I am done with the games the Eldar play with human lives. There is nothing that will bring me back into that never-ending war."

"That's a shame," Kahddria said. "Galad'Ysoysa named Duchess Julianna Taraen of House Kolmonen as his new Lord Morigahn."

Maxian's face went slack. At first his pale green eyes looked far away, not focusing on anything. Then he fixed those eyes on Kahddria. The look of scorn he had given Yrgaeshkil was nothing next to the raw fury Kahddria saw now.

"Damn you, Kahddria."

"I didn't do this," Kahddria said. "I didn't want this. I was content with the five still trapped away."

"Damn you, Kahddria" Maxian whispered. "And damn Grandfather Shadow."

His head sank, chin touching his chest. He stood there, a man defeated.

"I'm sorry," Kahddria said. "But if Grandfather Shadow is keeping himself hidden, you are the girl's only hope to learn what it means to be the Lord Morigahn." Kahddria wondered if she'd broken him. She'd given him something to care about again, something to lose. "I thought you didn't care?"

Maxian looked up. "Now I have to care."

The storm still raged in his eyes, but now he looked stronger, more determined than she'd ever seen any human before. His look frightened Kahddria even more than the thought of Galad'Ysoysa being free. The Greater Eldar had to be careful, as there were consequences for his actions. On the other hand, Maxian had the look of a desperate, cornered animal. He didn't care about consequences. For him, nothing was worse than he'd lived through, and after turning his back on the Eldar, death would only be a release into quiet oblivion.

"I will teach her," he said. "I will teach her things no Lord Morigahn has ever known. The world will shake with her coming, and once she's finished with the world, even the gods will tremble at her name."

TWO

Grandfather Shadow waited for all four Lesser Eldar and Maxian to leave the cave before he entered the World Between Worlds. The moment he left the physical realm, a force stronger than any power the God of Shadows could call upon pulled him into the King of Order's Realm.

Grandfather Shadow had hoped to forestall this moment a while longer – foolish as that notion was.

Every piece of the Realm of Order's clockwork menagerie glowed, destroying any chance for the existence of shadows or darkness. Everything in this realm moved in perfect precision. The gears and pulleys that kept all the worlds moving and working according to each one's natural laws clicked and whirred, creating a soothing harmony.

"GALAD'YSOYSA, YOUR FREEDOM HAS NOT BEEN PROPERLY EARNED," the King of Order's voice boomed from every corner of the realm.

"Your Majesty," Grandfather Shadow said. "The conditions for any of the Greater Eldar to earn freedom were very specific."

"IT WAS NOT THE PURE FAITH OF A MORTAL THAT FREED YOU."

"Begging Your Majesty's indulgence, your decree only specified the words be from a mortal's mouth. You did not specify the faith must be born from that same mortal's heart."

"ONE OF YOUR OWN SAENTS MANIPULATED THE WORDS IN ORDER TO ENSURE YOUR ESCAPE."

"And I'm sure that Your Majesty has punished him accordingly. I hope that you do not seek to blame me for the actions of my Saents while I was unable to control them."

There was a long pause. Grandfather Shadow began to fear he'd gone too far. If so, he'd sent Julianna to her death. Even with Faelin at her side, she could never hope to survive in the world as the Lord Morigahn without her god's aide.

"TAKE CARE, GALAD'YSOYSA, I AM CLOSE TO LOSING PATIENCE WITH YOU."

The gears, pulleys, springs, and cogs grew brighter, and the soft hum of their ceaseless work began to sound a bit more like a growl. Grandfather Shadow was treading on dangerous ground. He calculated quickly. The King of Order was already upset, and the twisting of words and logic that Grandfather Shadow would have to do in order to overcome this would likely upset the Incarnate even more.

"Your majesty is clearly too frustrated to continue this discussion in a rational manner. I request arbitration."

"VERY WELL," the King of Order replied. The suddenness of this compliance gave Grandfather Shadow a moment of pause. "LORDS OF JUDGEMENT, WE REQUIRE YOU."

A moment later, three cloaked figures appeared around Grandfather Shadow. The cloaks were three different colors: white, black, and gray.

The three spoke as one. "We have foreseen your need of us and have been watching events since the first moment that served as the catalyst for this argument. The King of Order brings his grievance. Proceed with your charges and arguments."

"GALAD'YSOYSA IS FREE FROM HIS PUNISHEMENT THROUGH GUILE AND TREACHERY, RATHER THAN PURE HUMAN-BORN FAITH. MORE TO THE POINT, THE ONE WHO FREED HIM IS NOT COMPLETELY HUMAN. I WOULD HAVE HIM PLACED BACK IN HIS PRISON AND THE WORDS OF MY EARLIER DECREE MODIFIED."

"Galad'Ysoysa," the Lords of Judgment spoke, "your counter."

"While I understand His Majesty's irritation, he should have taken more care with his words. For a Greater Eldar to win freedom, a mortal born no fewer than ten generations after you imprisoned us must call for a specific god with words of their own mouth, and those words must be born of pure faith. All those requirements were filled when Julianna called for me."

Laughter filled the Realm of Order. "YOUR OWN WORDS DAMN YOU. JULIANNA TARAEN IS NOT TRULY MORTAL."

Grandfather Shadow felt the unfamiliar sensation of worry creep into his stomach. He hadn't considered that. It might grow into panic if he were some other being, but he'd been manipulating gray areas since the world was new.

"I must politely disagree," Grandfather Shadow said. "She may not be human, but she is certainly mortal. Even with her mother's blood, Julianna will live out her life, perhaps a bit longer than those born about the same time as she, but nonetheless, her life span is finite. I believe that is the very definition of mortality."

"Enough." The Lords of Judgment each held their left hand up. "We understand The King of Order's grievance, and we know that Galad'Ysoysa will attempt to speak circles around any words used in argument against him. We will allow Julianna to determine the outcome of this discussion."

The Lords of Judgment vanished.

"THIS SHOULD BE INTERESTING."

"Indeed," Grandfather Shadow replied.

Without any preamble or word of dismissal, Grandfather Shadow found himself standing in his great hall in the celestial Realm of Shadows.

The chamber was a bit dusty but remained just as he had left it. He walked between twin rows of stone pillars to sit on his throne. Even though this return might be short-lived, Grandfather Shadow stretched out and settled into his rightful place. After a moment, it felt as if he'd never left. He waved his hand, and the Well of Knowledge appeared next to him. Misty water bubbled a bit inside the well.

Grandfather Shadow brushed the water with his fingertips and whispered, "The Lord Morigahn and Saent Faelin the Sentinel."

The water smoothed, flat as any mirror. An image formed. Two riders on a single black and white horse rode through a forest, rain pouring down upon them. The horse slowed and came to a stop a few moments later. Three cloaked figures – black, white, and gray – came out of the trees from different directions.

Grandfather Shadow waved his hand over the well. He could now hear the raindrops pattering on the ground and the wind in the trees.

"Julianna Taraen…"

THREE

Hours after leaving the Nightbrothers and Inquisitors behind, hopefully to kill each other, Julianna guided Vendyr between the trees at a slow walk. Rain came down in a steady drum, and Julianna let it fall on them. No need to give any possible survivors the means to track them.

Vendyr stopped in a small clearing. Julianna was so tired she hadn't realized he'd slowed until all forward movement stopped and the trees no longer wandered past them. She flicked the reins, but Vendyr wouldn't move.

Ahead to the right and left, two cloaked figures, one white and one gray, came out of the trees. She glanced over her shoulder and saw a third, this one wearing a black cloak. The cloaks were voluminous, like folded pavilions in the process of being unfurled in a strong wind.

"Julianna Taraen of House Kolmonen," the gray-cloaked man's voice was deep and full of command, "stand forward for judgment."

Julianna kicked Vendyr's flanks again, wanting him to ride the man down. She grew weary of people threatening her. One day, she would face her enemies without needing to run, but for now, she would have Vendyr trample him. The other two could be eliminated at another time. For some reason, she was sure she would see them both again.

Unfortunately, Vendyr would not move.

Taking a deep breath, Julianna drew on the dominion of Storms through the *Galad'fana*. Faelin's hand covered her mouth before she could speak.

"Don't." The command of Faelin's voice was as firm as his hand over her mouth, though Julianna could sense a bit of desperation in both his grip and tone. "Not with them. Those three stand greater than the gods. I'll explain later. Show deference and respect – but do not grovel."

Faelin slowly released his hand from Julianna's mouth. Then he slid off Vendyr.

"Forgive me, Great Lords of Judgment," Faelin said. "We are unfamiliar with the protocols for your proceedings."

"Speak plainly and honestly," the one in the white cloak said. "That is all we require of your charge, Sentinel."

"Faelin," Julianna asked, "what's going on?"

Faelin looked up at her. "These three are the Lords of Judgment. They preside over disputes within the celestial realms."

Julianna dismounted and faced the gray cloak. She couldn't see a face, just a pair of luminescent violet eyes.

"What do you want with me?" Julianna demanded. Her voice sounded much more confident than she felt, but that was the way of life for nobility. "I have no place among the celestials."

"You speak from ignorance," the black cloak said. "As with many laws, this does not absolve you of the crime."

"Your mother was not in any way human," the white cloak said. "Though her kind has forsaken the celestial realm, the power of their origins did not fade, nor did that choice mean you would not inherit that power to some degree."

"Ironic as it is, in granting upon you the title *Morigahnti'uljas*," gray cloak said, "Galad'Ysoysa has upset the balance of the Ykthae Accord. We are here to right that balance, one way or another."

"And how will you do that?" Julianna asked.

The three Lords of Judgment spoke together. "You stand at the crossroads of destiny. You must choose which path to take."

"What?" Julianna asked. "I thought destiny was fixed in the future, unchangeable. Isn't that why it's called destiny?"

"Not exactly," Faelin said. "Like everything else in creation, destiny is a dynamic force. It's not as if there is one fate for everything in the universe. Chance and freewill are just as powerful. If not, then there would be little point to life. All creatures know this, and that is why everything struggles against the world, because even taking fate into account, freewill and chance might play for or against our favor at any given moment."

Julianna placed her fists on her hips and fixed Faelin with her most practiced stare of authority. "And how is it you know all this, Faelin var-a'Traejyn."

"It's amazing what books you can find in libraries outside of the Kingdom's borders," Faelin replied.

He wasn't telling her everything, but that was fine – for now. She'd ask him about this later.

Taking a deep breath, Julianna faced the gray-cloaked figure.

"What are my choices?"

Again, they spoke as one. "Three paths stretch out before you: your father's, your mother's, and that of mediocrity."

"Why in the name of the five would anyone choose mediocrity?" Julianna asked.

"It is safe," Faelin said. "Well, as safe as life can be for a normal person."

"Will the Brotherhood of the Night and the Inquisitors continue to hunt me?" Julianna asked.

"Those are mortal institutions," the Lords of Judgment said.

"I can't bloody well then choose mediocrity can I?" Julianna said. "I'd be dead within a fortnight." She looked at Faelin. "Which should I choose?"

"The choice must be your own," the Lords of Judgment said.

Julianna closed her eyes. She breathed in and out in the same steady rhythm as she would have as if she were preparing for a duel.

Why couldn't things just be normal? Khellan should be alive. She should be planning a wedding with him that would infuriate her aunt. Alone in the darkness of her thoughts, Khellan's face smiled at her, eyes amused, handsome despite the scar running down his face. Julianna closed her eyes tighter, trying to hold back the grief as her throat tightened. Now she saw Khellan swinging from his *Galad'fana*, the scar twitching as he died. Soon, she only saw the scar in the darkness. Father had a scar like that too. Father had been the Lord Morigahn, while Mother had been at least partly a wolf and had given Julianna the ability to move backward and forward in time. That ability had saved Julianna time and again; she knew the power and understood how to use it. However, it hadn't helped her save Khellan or any of her other friends, but it had gotten her and Faelin away from the Brotherhood and Inquisitors.

Which path to choose?

Opening her eyes, Julianna drew her mother's dagger, the only thing she possessed from either of her parents. She turned it over and over in her hands, caressing the hilt, running her thumb and fingers over the single word etched on its blade.

Kostota.

She owed a great many people *kostota.* How best could she repay those debts? She couldn't with a life of mediocrity – not that she'd been considering that in the first place. That left Father or Mother? Mother or Father? *Kostota.* In the end, it all came down to that one word. She couldn't imagine any path where that did not lead to balancing her *kostota* with everyone.

Sheathing her dagger, Julianna faced the gray Lord of Judgment and made her choice.

The Lords of Judgment descended on her, cloaks billowing, eyes glowing madly in the gloom brought by the storm.

Being marked as the Lord Morigahn was a scratch compared to the anguish of having the essence of her soul remade.

FOUR

Grandfather Shadow watched from the Well of Knowledge throughout the night. At some point after the first hour, Julianna's voice grew so hoarse that her screams dried to croaks. She reached for Faelin, begging and pleading, but the Saent knew well that he could not help her. Julianna must suffer this alone. Not only would the Lords of Judgment strike Faelin down, this ordeal would teach Julianna to persevere and survive other great trials and suffering later.

The Lords of Judgment moved back from Julianna as dawn brought sunlight piercing through the storm clouds. Her nostrils flared with each ragged breath as she struggled to her feet, lips pressed tight together. After a moment, her knees steadied. She looked from one Lord of Judgment to the next. Her gazed settled on the gray-cloaked one. Julianna took a step forward and spat on him.

Grandfather Shadow laughed, full and deep. The sound filled his hall. He waved a hand over the Well of Knowledge, dismissing the scene. Julianna might not be what other people would call *fine*, and she would not know much of peace, but she would be counted amongst the greatest of those who bore the title of the Lord Morigahn. Yes, Grandfather Shadow had chosen well.

The laughter caught in his throat when he felt a familiar presence in his hall.

"What?" Grandfather Shadow asked. "The Lords of Judgment have made their decree based on Julianna's choice. Leave me be until I actually break the letter of the Ykthae Accord."

"I WILL ALLOW YOU TO RETURN TO YOUR GAMES, FOR NOW," the King of Order said. "HOWEVER, IF YOU DISPLEASE ME OVER MUCH, PERHAPS I'LL SEND YOU THROUGH THE CYCLE OF LIFE, DEATH, AND REBIRTH. HOW MANY OF YOUR ANCIENT ENEMIES WOULD LOVE TO FIND YOU AS A MORTAL?"

And with that, the King of Order was gone.

Grandfather Shadow stretched out on his throne. He was the only Greater Eldar free to roam the world, and that gave him an immense amount of power. For the moment, he could do as he pleased – so long as he didn't violate the King of Order's decrees. Grandfather Shadow understood the difference between bending the law and breaking the law, and he intended to bend as many celestial laws as possible – right up to the snapping point. The law was a lofty pedestal upon which the King of Order sat. If all those laws snapped at once, His Majesty could do nothing but fall. The moment that happened, Galad'Ysoysa would be ready to repay his thousand-year imprisonment.

"*Kostota na aen paras kostota,*" Grandfather Shadow whispered.

The words echoed in the hall, out through the windows, and into every shadow in existence.

Thus ends the first volume of

TEARS OF RAGE

Julianna's adventures continue in volume two

ONCE WE WERE LIKE WOLVES

About the Author

M Todd Gallowglas fell in love with writing with his first creative writing project assignment in third grade. He's been writing stories of magic and adventure ever since, and his brain seems to be wired to the fantastic when it comes to penning fiction. He has been a professional storyteller at Renaissance Faires and Medieval Festivals for twenty years. In 2009, he received his Bachelor of Arts in Creative Writing from San Francisco State University. He is a regular fiction contributor for the Call of Chthulu card game from Fantasy Flight Games, and writes several semi-regular blogs and on-line columns.

Find M Todd Gallowglas online at:

Blog: *www.mtoddgallowglas.com*
Facebook: *facebook.com/mgallowglas*
Twitter: *@MGallowglas*

11809600R00098

Made in the USA
San Bernardino, CA
30 May 2014